MACKINAC ISLAND CHRISTMAS

By Gail Gaymer Martin

Acknowledgements

Thank you to Tim Hygh, Executive Director, Mackinac Island Convention and Visitors Bureau for his help in locating a quality photograph of Main Street at Christmas. Thanks to the photographer, Sara Wright who provided the photograph of Main Street at Christmas for the book cover.

Chapter 1

Josie tossed her luggage on the bed and dropped to the edge of the mattress. A frown tugged her face as she pictured her friend Carol missing the ferry to the island. Carol should have arrived already, but she hadn't, and she hadn't called. Hopefully she would arrive late.

Or had she missed her friend's call? She dug into her pocket and pulled out her cell phone. No calls. She eyed her battery and saw it was at fifty percent. If Carol called, she should have received... Instead of speculating, she rose and headed back to the registration desk. Maybe the Inn had heard from her.

The woman smiled as she approached. "Did you forget something, or did I? I believe I gave you the Internet password, or—"

"Yes, you did. This is about my friend. She had planned to get here before me, but she's not here. I wonder if she'd called you."

She eyed the registration pad "Carol Abbott, right?"

Josie nodded and tried to read the log upside down. "I hope she remembered the name of the Inn. Carol can get muddled at times with her little one at the 'terrible twos' age." She grinned, and so did the woman at the desk.

"There are only a few hotels and Inns open this time of year. Why don't you call her?"

"Maybe I should, but I figured she was on the road. I'm sure she doesn't have Blue Tooth." She shrugged. "But I should try."

She stepped away from the desk and settled into a chair in the small lobby while she dialed her friend's number. She heard a click and saw that the connection didn't go through. She doubted that she needed the password in her phone for a call, but she pulled out the card the innkeeper had written it on and entered the numbers.

That didn't help either. She returned to the Innkeeper. "I'm not getting a connection. Do you know why?"

The woman shrugged. "Sadly, sometimes the weather's bad or the connections are bad. Go out on the porch and see if that works."

She did as the woman suggested, and sure enough, when she did connect, she tried Carol's number again, but it went to voice mail. She left a brief message, growing more concerned as time passed.

An accident. Was that it? Her chest tightened as her heartbeat jarred her chest. An accident? She released a ragged breath. No, it couldn't be.

She returned inside and turned to the desk. "I got through, but Carol's not answering so I suppose I'll wait and see what's happening."

"If your friend calls, I'll let you know. I'm sure she's okay. Delays happen sometimes, especially when children are involved."

Josie had never married, and she suspected with her lifelong attitude about marriage she would never have a child. She grinned thinking of what the woman at the desk said. "Delays happen sometimes, especially when children are involved." Under the circumstances, she faced that a delay was possible.

She rose and wandered to the door, stood a moment, and then stepped outside to the wide porch. The winter chill shivered down her back and limbs, and when she saw nothing, she stepped inside.

The innkeeper grinned. "You forgot how cold it is out there."

"I did. I don't know why I'm so concerned, but I looked forward to this time with Carol for a number of months. We've been good friends for so long, but she lives in the north and on the opposite side of Michigan so we rarely get together."

"And this was to be a special time." She came out from behind the desk. "I'm sure she'll arrive, and if not, you can still enjoy your time here. You know the Island is a special place. Dave and I have lived here a number of years, and we never tire of the seasons and the beauty of each."

"I've never been here in winter, and I have looked forward to seeing what an old-fashioned town is like during the winter and especially Christmas."

"It won't disappoint you, Josie." She extended her hand. "And by the way, I'm Rose. If you need anything please ask. Not everything is open, but enough businesses are available to meet most people's needs."

"Thanks so much, Rose. Worrying isn't getting me anywhere. I think I'll go up and put on something warmer and take a walk. I'll have my cell if she calls…or I should say when she calls."

Rose chuckled. "That's the way. Stay positive."

Instead of wasting time, she did as Rose suggested and returned to her room, unpacked, and looked out the window at the piles of snow still evident from the past week's snowfall. The island beckoned her to enjoy it. And anyway, she was starving. Breakfast was served at Cottage Inn, and from all Rose said, she looked forward to some of her excellent breakfasts, but lunch was on her own.

She eyed her phone again. Nothing. The lure of the Island drew her toward her jacket. She slipped it on, pulled up the hood and wrapped her neck in a scarf. Her gloves bulged from her pocket so she was ready. Downstairs, she waved goodbye to Rose and bounded down the steps turning left to head down Astor to Main Street.

Already Christmas decorations appeared wrapped around the old-fashioned lamp posts and garland wound with Christmas lights looped along the shop eaves. The Island closed at the end of October, but that didn't discourage visitors. Many enjoyed coming to the Island with fewer tourists and at a time that seemed more like a real town from the past—Victorian homes, horse and buggies, bicycles, and forts from the Revolutionary War and the War of 1812.

Her stomach growled as she admired the Mustang Lounge's Christmas lights ahead of her and smiled with the thought of finding food. Since the lights were on, she assumed they were open. When she reached the door, lights inside greeted her, and she stepped into the warmth and the scent of food.

A waiter motioned to an empty table nearby, and she slipped off her jacket and hung it on the back of the chair before sinking into it. When the waiter handed her a menu, she perused her options and settled on a Mustang Chef Salad with ham and turkey and all the fixings. The waiter returned with a glass of water, a cup and carafe of coffee.

He eyed her and she nodded. "Yes, regular black, and thanks. She ordered the salad, and then sipped the hot coffee as he headed away. Her gaze drifted to the old hewn wood walls and areas covered with logs, she guessed had been cut from the Island trees. Much of the Island remained woods with dirt roads winding through to various historical locations. The only thing that ruined the moment was her concern for Carol.

A long sigh emptied her lungs, and she pulled out her phone again and hit Facebook. She scanned the messages of people she knew and most whom she didn't but had accepted as friends. The idea made her grin. She lifted the coffee again, feeling the swirl of warmth rising from the cup and took another sip.

"Is this your jacket?"

She jumped, hearing someone behind her. When she turned, a man held up her jacket and arched his brow. "It was on the floor behind you."

"Thanks. It's mine." She leaned forward as he lapped it over the seat back again. "I didn't feel it fall, but then I was too intrigued with the history in this building."

He moved around to her side. "It's one of the oldest buildings on the Island. Dated to the 1780s, and I've heard it's the oldest tavern in Michigan. That makes it very special, I've always thought."

"The Island is very special. Obviously, I'm a tourist and though I've been on Mackinac Island many times, I've never been here in winter." She extended her hand. "By the way, I'm Josie Ryan from Royal Oak. It's a suburb of Detroit."

"I know where it is. I've lived in Birmingham for years." He grasped her fingers in his. "I'm Christopher Banks, but everyone calls me Chris."

"Hi, Chris. Would you like to join me?"

"I was hoping you'd ask." He grinned and slipped into a seat adjacent to hers. "Are you here alone?"

Her pulse jumped. "Not by choice. I'm supposed to meet a friend, but as you can see I am alone."

"I'm sorry. Maybe he—"

"It's a she." Josie shook her head. "Carol's a long-time friend who I haven't seen in a few years, and we made these plans months ago, so I am at a loss. I keep worrying that something—"

"Lots of things can happen. She missed the ferry. She had a flat on the way, and it takes a while for someone to get to her on the freeway. It could be lots of things that—"

"I know. I keep telling myself the same thing, but it isn't like her not to call."

He patted her arm. "Just pray that she's okay and then wait and see."

"I wish I were more like you." She managed to grin although her heart wasn't in it.

The waiter returned. "Your salad will be ready shortly." He refilled her coffee cup and took Chris's order of a Crispy Chicken Club sandwich, then left.

"I'll have to try that." Josie smiled. "A crispy chicken club sounds yummy."

He leaned back. "If you're here long enough, you can try lots of things. This is one of the few places open for meals."

She shrugged. "I like it here. So far anyway." As she finished, her cell phone lilted its song, and she grasped it off the table and eyed the caller. "It's her. Thank you, God." She hit the button. "Carol, where are you?"

She closed her eyes listening to Carol's story, grateful that she was okay but now worried about her two-year-old. "Do they know what it is?"

Amidst her friend's quaking voice, she tried to understand what she said. "Carol, I'm so sorry but you're at a good hospital, and I'm relieved that you weren't in an accident or something. I've been worried since I got here."

After the words were out of her mouth, she regretted it. "I'm not upset with you. Goodness, if I had been in your situation, I wouldn't have thought of anything but my child, and I know that certain parts of the hospital restrict the use of cell phones. Please keep me informed, and I'll—"

Carol's next question, at this point, had no answer. "I'm not sure. I'll probably stay a couple of days and then leave. It's not as fun to sightsee alone." As the words exited, she looked into Chris's eyes. He didn't flinch with her comment. Though telling Carol, she wasn't alone at the moment came to mind, it would take too much explanation, and it wasn't important. Chris was a nice man who picked up her jacket from the floor.

"Okay, do that. I'll be thinking of you and little Jacob. He's such a cutie, and it's hard to picture him that ill. Prayers that they find an answer quickly, Carol. Love you both." She pressed the off button and set her phone on the table. "As you could hear, Carol's two-year-old is very ill and at this point they don't know what's wrong."

"I'm sorry, Josie. I'm sorry for them, and for you. I know you're concerned but now you've been sort of stranded here, although—"

"Being alone isn't really the problem. I can cut my vacation short, and I probably will, since I don't know anyone—"

"How about this? I'm here for a while visiting my granddad. He had been very ill but is doing much better now. I decided to stay to give him a chance to heal and feel confident about being alone again. I can work from here since much of my job involves the computer."

"That's a bonus. I'm an English instructor at the university. I had three weeks vacation due because I did some extra projects when I should have been on vacation, and then we have the holidays off to the New Year so it was a perfect time to come here and not feel rushed."

"Sure is."

"I had planned to go home for Christmas, although my parents live in Florida. They come to Michigan in the summer. So I suppose I really have no reason to rush home, and I'd also love to be here for Christmas. As you can tell, I can be wishy washy since changing plans isn't easy for me."

"I think it's that way for many of us. You knew what you wanted to do and how you'd spend your time, and now your plans have been waylaid. That means you have to make new decisions, and on that note, I'm a great Island guide. Gramps has lived here most of his life, and I spent the summers here and sometimes even came for Christmas, so I'm your man, and I charge very little."

Her head drew back before she could stop it. "What is your—"

He tilted his head back and chuckled. "What is the charge? Zero. I love the Island and enjoy seeing everything again and again. I was teasing, but then you don't know my sense of humor."

He'd said that right. Her imagination had sent her to a bad place until her senses returned. "I could buy you dinner. How's that?"

"Does that mean you accept my offer?"

Did it? The words had just flown out. "I don't expect you to spend every moment with me. I can do many things by myself. I know they have buggy tours, and—"

"Most buggies are taxis at this time of year, but we have snowmobiles. They are the exception to the rule that there are no personal motorized vehicles on the Island. The citizens that live here year round need a way to get to St. Ignace once the snow bridge is ready. It saves them flying over and back with groceries."

She'd struggled not to let her embarrassment show, even though heat raced up her chest to her neck. She knew so little about the workings of the Island. "I know I've heard that, but it's such a different way of life than I'm used to. I'm just a tourist."

"Don't say that. The Island remains as it is because of tourists…and I suppose a kind of historical pride. And that's what makes the Island so enchanting. I think that's what they call it."

She nodded. "It is charming to me."

The waiter finally appeared with both meals, and it struck her that the salad had taken as long to make as a four-course dinner, but then, what did it matter. She had nowhere to go.

"Sorry." The waiter set her salad in front of her and then placed Chris's sandwich in front of him. "We had a slight problem in the kitchen. Normally these meals don't take this long."

"It's okay." But it was strange. Still his expression reflected his discomfort, and she wanted to be easy on the guy. He wasn't the cook. "I'm still hungry."

"Thanks." He stood back. I'll bring you some fresh coffee and a meal discount for next time."

She shrugged. "It's not necessary."

"But it is. We want you to come back." He sent her a big smile, and so did Chris.

The man turned away, and in moments returned with the coffee and a discount card that impressed her.

Chris leaned over to view the card. "Looks like you'll have to bring someone along with you."

"It does look like it." She grinned and handed it to him. "You can hang on to it."

"But only if you promise to come back here with me."

Thinking of the many good food choices on the menu, she didn't have to think. "I'd be happy to."

He took the card and slipped it into his wallet. "Let's eat and then we can take a walk. It's a nice day, and I don't think it will get too cold before the sun goes down."

"I hope not." She lifted her fork and delved into the salad piled high with the meat and greens. For the first time since she could remember, Chris had offered her something she usually didn't do, and that was being adventuresome. The man made her comfortable, and to her surprise, she trusted him. Now all she could do is hope that she hadn't been fooled by his seeming kindness.

♥

Trying to be subtle, Chris studied Josie's face. She was very pretty, and though she sounded intelligent, she had a bit of vulnerability that he didn't understand, as if she needed her plans to keep her moving in the right direction. He hoped to give her a taste of adventure. It was something he enjoyed, those spur of the moment plans that frequently offered the best times.

She delved into the salad with relish while he took a big bite of his sandwich. They'd talked and waited long enough to put an edge on their hunger.

Josie set down her fork and lifted her head. "This is delicious, but I'm getting full. Tell me about you. I know you have a grandfather here on the island, and since you're here to give him support, I'll make the assumption you're a pretty nice guy." She noticed his ring finger was bare. "I assume you're not married."

His head jerked upward before he could stop it. "Right. I can't image that I would have asked to sit with you if I had been." He grinned at his honesty. "Not that I had anything in mind, but I probably would have felt as if it wasn't appropriate." He shrugged hoping what he said made sense to her.

"I get you. And I didn't think the coat was a come-on. You're a nice guy as I said."

"Thanks. How about telling me about you?"

She raised her hand to stop him. "Hang on. All I've

learned is you're not married, and I really didn't think you were since you're not wearing a ring."

He eyed his left hand and shook his head. "Do we all do that?"

"What?"

"Check out ring fingers?"

"I thought only women did that."

He pressed his lips together to stop another smile. "I think men do too."

"That's a new piece of information." Josie leaned back in silence.

"You're waiting for more?"

She nodded. "I'm curious."

"So am I." He rested his elbows on the table and thought a moment. "Let's see, you mentioned your parents. Mine live in Michigan. My dad still works even though he could have retired years ago, but he has no hobbies and I think my mom has encouraged him to work rather than be hanging around the house like a couch potato."

Josie grinned. "I'm glad my parents decided to move to Florida. They golf, belong to a social club in their community where they attend parties, play cards and games. Mom belongs to a book club, and Dad hangs out with the men around the TV for every sport you could name."

He chuckled, wondering why his father didn't seem to be a sports fan. "That sounds healthy."

She eased back again and used two fingers to mime zipping her mouth. He got the point.

"I suppose the biggest thing about me is that I'm guardian to my brother's daughter."

She straightened her back, her eyes wide. "His

daughter? Why? What happened?"

The lump in his throat always surprised him. Two years ago, my younger brother Gary and his wife Mindy were involved in a drunk driver accident. Thank the Lord Ellie was with my parents. Gary and Mindy both died. The driver of the other car is in prison for another year or so. It's not enough." Moisture rimmed her golden brown eyes, and his chest tightened.

"I agree, Chris. Losing two people you love had to be horrible, and I multiple that by a hundred when you said they have a young child. It's heartbreaking. I'm grateful she wasn't with them."

Her voice broke with the same emotion he experienced. "Ellie's four now. A sweet little girl. She'll be five in February . I can't believe it."

"Is she with you on the Island?"

Her question squeezed his heart. "No, she's visiting her maternal grandparents. I thought she might find the Island boring since there are few kids and—"

"Boring?" Josie's eyes widened, and her gazed captured his. "Being with you wouldn't be boring, and the Island is so different. Horse and buggies. No cars. New places. And I'm sure more snow will fall soon."

"It will. Actually, she'd love that. I did think about it now that I'm here. She would love to ride in the snowmobiles. She's quite adventuresome."

"Then why not have them bring her here, or have someone else bring her here. If you're staying for Christmas, she'll miss you. Don't you think?"

As the question left her, she drew back and covered her mouth with her hand. He studied her a minute, unable to fathom what bothered her. "Is something wrong?"

"Yes, me. I'm sorry, Chris. You made the decision to send her to her grandparents, and it's really not my business."

He reached over and touched her hand. "But you made a good point, Josie."

"I shouldn't have made any point."

"But you did, and I'm grateful. I've felt uneasy for the past few days when I think about her. I wished I hadn't made that decision. I'm afraid it's too late now though. Her grandparents won't bring her up. I know them too well."

She opened her mouth and closed it. Instead, she only nodded. "Maybe next time you come."

Though his heart still weighted, he nodded. "Next time."

He finished his sandwich while Josie pushed her salad around in the bowl and finally picked up a forkful. When she finished, she placed the fork on the bowl and took a drink of water, lifting her eyes to his with a grin. "This salad is way too big for me."

"They'll box it, and you can have it tomorrow."

"I'm staying at Cottage Inn. I doubt she wants my leftovers in her refrigerator."

"Then bring it along. I'll put it in Gramp's. He won't mind, and you can have it tomorrow."

She squinted at him as if he were out of his mind. "I don't think—"

That's right. Don't think. Just do it." He chuckled, and she joined him. "Here's an idea. Let's go to Gramps' but first I promised to pick up some fudge. That's his only vice."

"A vice?" Her smile grew.

"I tease him, but I still buy it for him. He's in good

health. You'll see."

He flagged the waiter for the bill and a box for Josie's salad. When she'd salvaged the leftovers and put the box into the small bag that the waiter gave her, he paid the bill. While she tried to give him money, he waved her hand away and beckoned her to follow him. He'd never been quite so forward with a woman, but he liked Josie, and she needed a friend.

So did he.

Chapter 2

Josie followed Chris as if he were the Pied Piper. She'd never been so trusting with a stranger, but something about the Island gave her a sense of safety and spirit. Without her friend Carol joining her, she would have been lost, and there he was, a man who'd come to her rescue without knowing it.

As they headed to Main Street, snowflakes floated from the sky like white moths, settling here and there, and then vanishing. A few twirled along the sidewalk and some settled on a patch of frozen snow left from days earlier. She drew her scarf around her neck and tucked her free hand into her pocket rather than dig out her gloves although the hand froze that carried the sack with the salad.

Chris pointed out a few stores that were open as they trekked along toward the fudge shop. She was grateful when they reached the store, but her spirit dropped when she read the closed sign hung on the door.

Chris shook his head and shrugged. "I guess

Gramps will have to live without his fudge." As he turned, a rap sounded on the window, and he spun back around.

"Did you want fudge?" A woman stood in the doorway.

"Yes. My gramps had his heart set on it, but if you're closed I—"

"I'm closing now, but come in. I'll leave the closed sign up." She beckoned them to go inside.

When they entered, the warmth eased Josie's chattering teeth. The chill had been unexpected, perhaps a foolish assertion, but earlier in the morning, the bright sun gave a pleasant warmth to the air, and she forgot that as clouds decide to roll in so does the temperature.

"I think Gramps would love the chocolate with macadamian nuts, and this young woman would enjoy…" Chris gazed at her with a grin. "It's your pick."

Josie eyed the many options and chose. "How about the peanut butter?"

He chuckled. "Other than chocolate, that's my next favorite." He gave a nod to the clerk, and she boxed and bagged the treats. After Chris paid and picked up the two bags, he paused. "Thanks for opening up. I appreciate it and so will Gramps."

The woman grinned. "You're welcome, and I hope Gramps enjoys it."

"He will." Chris turned toward the door and Josie followed him.

Outside the same cold chill ran up her spine. Chris gave her a questioning look and slipped his arm around her back. "You need a warmer coat. I hope you have one."

"Probably not, but I have a couple of heavy sweaters, and I can layer."

"Good thinking. But we do have a walk to the house, so I'll keep my arm around you if that's okay."

The warmth of his body next to hers helped the chill, and she agreed it was fine. In fact, even without the warmth, she enjoyed the feeling of a strong man holding her close. Those experiences were rare since she'd watched the failed marriages of her two sisters and wanted no part of matrimony. Commitment that worked seemed only for a romance novel.

Chris picked up his steps, and she hurried along anxious to get out of the cold. When they reached French Lane, he pointed to his granddad's house, a gray two-story home with red shutters and encircled by a picket fence that gave it a homey look.

She strolled beside Chris to the porch, and when he opened the door, a welcoming flood of heat greeted her. Inside, the comfortable furniture added a homey look, and when Chris called out that he was home, a trim grey-haired gentleman ambled through the doorway and stopped. "I knew you to bring home stray dogs when you were young, but never a lovely young woman." He stepped toward her, his hand extended. "I'm Chris's grandfather, Harold Banks."

"Very nice to meet you, Mr. Banks. I'm Josie Ryan—Joselyn, actually."

"Okay, Gramps. You just learned something I didn't know. Joselyn. That's a pretty name." Chris squeezed her arm.

His grandfather gave her a wink. "My grandson thinks he can learn everything about a woman in a couple of hours. You see that's his problem. A woman is mysterious and needs more time to reveal everything you'd like to know, Chris."

Chris chuckled, but his grandfather had probably spoken more truth than even Chris realized. "I think you're right, Mr. Banks."

"Oh come now. How about calling me Harry?"

Harry seemed too familiar, but she agreed. Before she had to find something else to say, Chris handed his grandfather the bag holding the fudge, and Harry gave a headshake and peeked inside. "Chocolate with my favorite nuts. Good for you, Chris." Then he noticed the other sack. "And what do we have there?" He motioned toward the other bag.

Chris gave a head nod to her. "Our guest likes peanut butter, and by the way—he reached toward her other package—she has left over salad from Mustang Lounge so I told her I'd store it here for her."

She studied him a moment, confused as to why she'd agreed to take the leftover, but since she had it, she handed him the bag. "It was a good salad."

Harry nodded. "Then don't throw something good away. That's my philosophy. I was born after the depression, but my parents didn't forget the horror of it, and we saved everything. Mom would make soup out of leftovers or some kind of casserole when we salvaged enough. Those were the days when moms had to be creative."

Josie's chest tightened, unable to imagine life back then. "I'm sure it was horrible for everyone. My mom's mother remembered. Once in a while, Grandma would say something to remind us of how blessed we were."

Harry beckoned her. "Don't just stand there. Come

in." He motioned to the sofa and easy chairs. "Are you here visiting family?"

She settled on the sofa and told him about Carol and her former plans. "I decided to stay a few days anyway. I've looked forward to being on the Island during the Christmas season for a long time."

"Then stay as long as you want. People are friendly, and it looks as if Chris has offered to be your guide around the island."

Her pulse skipped. "Yes, he was nice enough to offer, but I don't want to take advantage of—"

"Chris will enjoy your company. I have no doubt. Otherwise he's stuck with me or Agnes Coleman next door. She has her eye on him for her granddaughter."

Chris shook his head and sank onto the other end of the sofa. "Gramps, let her know that I'm not looking for anyone unless it's someone I connect with myself. I don't believe in blind dates or matchmakers."

Harry slapped his knee. "I can tell her, and I have, but that woman is about as deaf as a stuffed moose head, except she hears only what she wants to."

Josie chuckled at Chris's expression when he heard his grandfather's explanation. "That's another thing about women and men too. I think it's called selective hearing."

"There you go." Harry clapped his hands and sank into a recliner. "I can see why Chris brought you home. You're a woman who can make people smile, and we like that around here."

She wasn't sure if she should thank him or just let the comment drop, but she gave a quick nod as she gazed at both of them while an uneasy feeling crept up her back. "I should head back to the motel, I suppose."

"Why?"

Harry's arched brow jolted her as much as the question. "No particular reason, but I don't want to interfere—"

"Interfere? Chris, is this lovely young woman interfering with your plans?" Harry tilted his head toward his grandson.

"No, Gramps. I have no plans."

Harry straightened his back. "No plans. Why rush off? You and Chris could take a ride. or we could play a game, or—"

"A ride sounds like a good idea, Gramps. I'll pull out the snowmobile and give Josie a look at the Island in winter." He rose and then came to a full stop. "But she doesn't have a heavy jacket. Do we have an extra one around here?"

"Sure do." Harry popped up like a Jack-in-the-box.

Her mouth hung open, watching him charge across the room and through the doorway. "Your granddad can move with the speed of lightning."

Chris grinned as he shook his head. "I know. When I was a kid and tried to get away with anything, I thought Gramps sprouted wings." His brow wrinkled before he turned his head. "I have no idea what he's going to bring you. If it's something weird, you don't have to wear it."

Harry appeared before she had to comment and handed her a dark blue down filled jacket with a hood lined with white fur. "Belongs to my cousin, Rosie, who left it here so she didn't have to lug it to the Island if she came in winter. She said anyone could use it, but I thought the offer would go unneeded until today."

She eyed the good-looking coat. As she stuck out

her arm to try it on, Chris took it from her and held it open so she could slip in more easily. "Thanks." The jacket fit as if it were hers. "Perfect."

Chris gave a nod. "It looks great, and it should keep you warm."

"We have a couple pairs of ladies boots in the back closet, Chris. One might fit Josie if you want to take a look."

Her eyes widened, hearing that Harry seemed to have everything to provide her with a warm and comfortable day in the snow. She followed Chris to the back of the house, and when her foot slipped into the boot without a problem, her breath left her. The situation arrived like a surprise gift out of nowhere. Who would have thought?

"You and your granddad amaze me, Chris."

"He always amazes me. That's why I love to visit him. Gramps is somehow full of surprises. I'd be surprised if he wasn't."

She grinned at his twisted comment. "You both surprise me, but even more you make me very grateful. I realize now I didn't come prepared. I'm not sure what I was thinking about winter in the North and on an Island, but whatever I was thinking was wrong."

He shifted to her side and slipped his arm around her back. "A new experience. From now on, you'll be an old hand dealing with a northern winter."

"I hope so. Next time I may not find a Fairy Godfather to take care of me."

"Is that Gramps or me?"

"You pick." She chucked his chin as he laughed.

With the warm jacket and boots, Chris went outside and pulled the snowmobile from the large storage shed.

When he brought it up to the house, she stepped onto the back porch while Harry watched them from the doorway.

She settled into the seat behind him, slipped on the gloves she'd had in her jacket pocket and pulled up the furry hood. Chris had changed his clothes too, wearing bibbed pants and an insulated jacket similar to hers. He wore a helmet and handed her one. "We don't move without a helmet."

He'd made his point, and she slipped it on over her head and tightened the straps.

"Keep your feet flat on the running board, hang on to the handgrips, and lean in the direction I do when we're making a turn." He twisted around and gave her a wink. "Ready?"

"As ready as I'll ever be." She winked back.

"Here we go." He stepped on the pedal and the machine shot forward.

She hung on, praying she wouldn't fly out of the thing, but once he reached the road, he slowed and grinned. "Just testing your stamina."

"It's very weak. Be kind."

Chris reached over and patted her hand. "I'm always kind."

He leaned his body to the left, and she followed as the snowmobile glided to the road. The wind whipped past her, sneaking inside her hood and ruffling her hair. She'd forgotten to tie the string to hold her hood on tighter but couldn't let go of the handgrips so she put up with the situation until he decided to stop.

He headed up Cadette Road and past the Grand Hotel, a massive beauty, with columns on the longest front porch ever made, she'd been told. The beautiful building had been used in movies and drew thousands of tourists a year to take a look as well as many visitors who enjoyed their stay in the lovely hotel.

After they passed the hotel, Chris continued up Grand Avenue and then made a right on Huron. The streets became rougher dirt roads heading into the well-known historic area of the Island. The snow sailed past captured by the winter breeze and the movement of the snowmobile. Flakes caught on her eyelashes and the cold penetrated any spot not covered by the down filled jacket or boots.

"Ahead you'll see Fort Holmes made of earth and logs. The Island has two forts. You know the big one on Main Street, Fort Mackinac, but this one was built by the British during the War of 1812. It's on the highest elevation of Mackinac Island and was used as a lookout against enemies."

He came to a stop beside the fort. "You'll notice it's in bad decay. I hear they're going to rebuild it to look just like it did when it was new."

"I'm sure it takes a lot of work to keep the antique structures intact." With the pause, she let go of the handgrips and tightened the string around the hood to protect her frozen ears. "What else is in this area."

"We'll go to Arch Rock. The view is interesting. It's also a historic location, and it's one of the reasons, the Island became Mackinac National Park and later a state park too."

"Chris, you're a walking encyclopedia."

He grinned. "When I'm here alone with only Gramps, I don't do much except visit the island locations and learn the history. Maybe I should live here and be a tour guide."

"Maybe you should."

He shook his head. "This is more fun. I'd rather take a friend along with me."

A friend. The reference sent prickles down her arms. He made a good friend, even though sadly, the friendship would be short lived. "I'm glad I benefit from your preference."

His eyes met hers, and she sat frozen in space, not from the cold but from the amazing look in his milk chocolate eyes.

When he shook his head as if waking up, he glanced at his watch. "Whoa. Do you realize it's getting late. The sun will be down shortly, and we need to get back. It'll be dinner time."

She adjusted her feet and grasped the handgrips as he started the motor and turned toward the road. "I had lots more to show you but that'll have to wait for another day."

Another day. Her old plans turned white and melted into the snow. Today a whole new set of plans had appeared, and her earlier disappointment brightened. Things often happened for the best. Today had proven it.

♥

Chris stared at his cell phone he'd put on the dresser. No matter how hard he tried, Josie's concern hammered in his head. "If you're staying for Christmas, she'll miss you. Don't you think?" Yes, Ellie would miss him, and he would miss her. He shook his head, wishing he could get his thought in order. He needed Josie's organizational skills. Besides beauty, she had brains and seemed to think things through.

He leaned forward and lifted his phone, eyeing it as

he leaned back. Who should he call is the next question. Ellie was with her mom Mindy's parents, and he was certain that they wouldn't bring her to the Island. If they would bring her as far as the ferry, he would gladly meet anyone in Mackinaw City or if they preferred in St. Ignace in the Upper Peninsula. Either one.

Common sense said he had to talk with Mindy's parent's first. He moved through the contact list, closed his eyes a moment, and then opened them to press the connection. The phone rang. Once, twice, three times. Ready to give up, he lowered his hand and heard a click and a hello.

"Hi, this is Chris. Since I've been on Mackinac Island, I realize that not bringing Ellie was probably a mistake. She would love it here with the horses and growing snow piles. So would it disappoint you if she came here to spend Christmas with me."

The man's tone snapped asking the question he expected. "You expect us to drive over two-hundred miles because you changed your mind? I don't think so, Chris. We'll manage with Ellie here for Christmas. We have plans, but we'll get a sitter."

They have plans for Christmas and Ellie will be with a sitter? That was no Christmas for a four year old child who lost her parents. He cringed. He'd made the horrible mistake thinking it was for the best. He'd been so wrong. "Mr. Rodman, I'll see if I can make other arrangements. That will save you finding a sitter for Ellie. I'll get back to you."

Before Rodman had a chance to respond, Chris hit the end button and tossed himself back in the chair. Now what? His pulse beat like a tom-tom and rattled in his head. He'd go back if he had to, but... He sat a moment and relaxed as an idea struck him.

With no need to look up the number, he pressed his choice, and when it clicked, he heard his Mom's voice. "Chris here, Mom."

"What's wrong?"

He shook his head, knowing that would be his mother's first concern. "Nothing, Mom. I made a big mistake not bringing Ellie, and I called Mindy's parents to see if they would bring her to the Island or at least to the ferry where I can bring her to the Island. And when I asked—"

"They refused, right?"

"You're correct." He faltered, but told her about the baby sitter and the attitude. "So guess what I'm calling about."

"Hmm." She chuckled. "I'm glad you did. Ellie needs a Christmas and not a baby sitter. I'll talk to your dad, but I don't think it's a problem. We can drive up there and maybe spend the night before we go back."

"That's great, Mom. Gramps will love to see you, and if you and Dad are willing, I'd be so grateful."

"We need to see your granddad anyway. It's been a while."

She made a chuckle noise and that threw him, as well as caused him to be suspect.

"So why the change in plans?"

Yep, there it was. "Well...I-I see the snow and the Christmas decorations, plus the horses and—"

"What's her name?"

He drew back and stared at the phone a moment. "What does that mean?"

"The change of heart seems as if it might have come from a woman's encouragement."

"Do you think I can't have a change of heart, Mom?

"No, but changing your decision when you're already there and had given it earlier thought is rare. Something influenced your thinking, I would say."

His mother knew him too well. "Okay, Mom. Her name is Joselyn, but she goes by Josie. She came here to spend time with a lady friend for a few days, but her lady friend's child got sick at the last minute, and she couldn't come. I met Josie eating alone in a restaurant." He finished the details, but as always his mother's ability to read her kids minds amazed him. She did that to his younger brother too, before he...

She chuckled at his silence. "Sorry, Chris, but I think mothers have a sixth sense or just the ability to read unspoken words."

"You can say that again, Mom." He drew in a breath, both relieved and astounded. "Will you let me know what Dad says and when you'll come up...if you will?"

"We will, I'm sure, but I'll call you with a date. Tell Gramps we'll see him too, okay?"

"I will, and you'll meet Josie. She's a very nice woman."

"I look forward to it."

So did he, and as much, he looked forward to having Ellie with him for Christmas. Next time, he would think things through far better than he had this time.

Chapter 3

Josie rolled over, adjusted her pillow and gazed at her pleasant room at Cottage Inn. Her plan had gone full circle. With Carol, she'd pictured taking a taxi tour, walking down Main Street admiring the Christmas decorations, shopping, and perhaps checking out the library, but most of her time would have been socializing with her dear friend she rarely saw. And now her plan had turned into a very different and new situation. Yet in the process, she'd found a new friendship in Chris, and a new acquaintance in the form of his grandfather Harry, who had become quite an interesting character.

Chris's smile had brightened the past few days and left her curious. Today she hoped to get him to confess what was on his mind. She'd heard from Harry that in the evening the Christmas Tree would be lighted in the center of Main Street. Other festivities would occur too, and tomorrow the Christmas Bazaar would begin, a fund raiser for the medical center and some of the churches. The series of events lifted her spirit. She'd never experienced small town living, and she liked the friendly feeling.

When her cell phone rang, she jumped and checked the time, wondering what was wrong. She spotted Chris's phone number, and all she could think of was his grandfather had a setback.

"Good morning, Chris. What's wrong?"

"Wrong? Nothing." Silence filled the air for a moment. "Sorry, I didn't realize it was so early. I'm taking Gramps to breakfast for a treat. He rarely eats out and wondered if you'd like to join us."

"I'd love to, but Rose prepares a breakfast for her guests, and I should tell her ahead of time if I'm not eating."

"Ah. I forgot about that."

"I'll see you later though if you'd like."

"If I'd like? You know I would. Dress warm. We can go out on the snowmobile and later they're having the Christmas tree lighting plus more."

"I know about the tree lighting, but what's the plus more?"

"A surprise. Just do as I suggest and dress warm."

She grinned at her phone. "Okay, boss. I'll see you later." She clicked off and slipped her legs over the mattress. Today sounded like a fun day, but as she considered all the plans they were making, she realized that she had to go home eventually. With all the changes, she'd now left her plans open ended. Yet one day she had to face that after the holidays, she had to return to work.

Forcing herself to rise, she headed into the bathroom to shower and dress. Chris said to dress warm, and she should have brought some heavier clothing, but she still had the jacket he'd loaned her so that would keep the top of her warm…and the boots.

At breakfast, Rose had prepared a large casserole of eggs, bacon, cheese and cubed bread. It smelled delicious, and she took a large spoonful. Being outdoors so much had whetted her appetite, and if she didn't want to put on pounds, she needed to exercise. Maybe they could walk today.

"I'm glad you found someone to spend time with, Josie. I'm sure when your friend couldn't make it, you were disappointed."

"I was and really I still am. I looked forward to seeing her and having some quality time, but yes, I'm glad I met Chris. He's a very nice man, and his granddad is also interesting. It's not the plans I had in mind, but I'm seeing the island and—"

"He's also a good-looking guy. Haven't you noticed?"

She eyed Rose and saw a silly grin on her face. "I did notice, but I'm trying to ignore that aspect of him. We're new-found friends, and I'm very comfortable with him for the two of us basically being strangers."

"That's nice, but I wonder how long you can keep up the pretense."

Pretense? She thought a moment. "I'm not pretending he's not a handsome guy. What I'm doing is focusing on his personality. He's very thoughtful and kind. I feel comfortable with him, especially since we just met and—"

"Those attributes are important. No question about that. I think relationships can't be built on looks alone. If we're going to commit to someone, it has to be based on those things you mentioned. I agree."

Josie studied Rose, confused by her comments. Did she think that she and Chris were involved and just not admitting it or did she… Forget it. "I think we're going to the tree lighting tonight. That should be fun."

"Everyone is there. It is a good time for the town. I hope you enjoy singing."

"Singing?"

"They have a carol sing around the tree."

She grinned. "I love this. I enjoy the carols. Everything is like a fairytale here."

Rose patted her shoulder. "I'm glad you're enjoying it despite the plan change. Lots to do here at Christmas and New Years. You'll see."

Back in her room, Josie settled into the chair and leaned back with Chris on her mind. She considered him a friend, but she found herself playing games with that term just as Rose had said. He was a wonderful man, and she was surprised that he was single, but then people are often surprised that's she's single. And Rose was also correct about what makes a solid commitment, not just good looks, but good attributes that bring out the best in people, even when times get tough. She had to admit that her parents were both thoughtful and kind. They were more socially active than she'd ever been. So what had influenced her?

Her cell phone rang, and when she looked at the caller, she recognized Chris's phone number. "Hi, what's up?"

"We're back from breakfast so I thought you might like to either walk around town or take out the snowmobile again."

"I'll take you up on the walk. If I'm going to spend time here, I need some warmer clothes. I think a place on Main Street sells what I need." She hoped.

"I know the place. It's Mackinac Outfitter near the ferry dock. I'll come to Cottage Inn—"

"No need. Let's meet there. It's closer for you, and I'm ready."

"Okay. See you soon."

She heard the disconnect and rose, thankful that she'd thought about her lack of warm clothing today and not later. The events coming up, like singing carols and seeing the tree lighting, meant standing outside at night in the cold. She grinned, picturing Chris on the way to meet her.

The day already held a chill, and the cloud-filled sky hinted at more snow. She hurried along Astor to Main Street, and when she turned, the ferry docks were only a long block away. Before she reached it, Chris stood outside the Mackinac Outfitter building and waved as he walked toward her.

"Good morning, and thanks for meeting me. I knew I needed something warmer, but you can help."

"I can?" He arched his eyebrow.

"Okay, silly. I mean you have a better idea what I need to keep warm."

He slipped his arm around her back and pulled her closer. "How's this?"

It was great, but logic said she needed more. "Nice, but impossible on the snowmobile."

He dropped his shoulders with a dramatic flair. "I guess you're right."

She couldn't help but laugh at his antics. "I hope they're open." He left his arm where it had been and led her to the doorway as he pointed to the Open sign. "I checked."

She slipped her arm around his waist and squeezed. "Thank you."

Chris pushed open the door, and she dropped her arm as she stepped into the warmth of the shop. "Wow. They have lots of choices here."

"That's why they're called 'Outfitters.'"

She poked him with her elbow. "Thanks for the information." Ignoring his playfulness, she wandered down the aisles, looking for some style of warm pants, and she needed heavy socks to wear with the boots.

"Here you go." He beckoned her to a row of bibbed insulated snow pants.

"Perfect." Scanning the colors, she selected blue since it was similar to the blue jacket she'd borrowed from Chris. She checked the price—expensive but not bad—and worth it. "Heavy socks, and if I can use the jacket you loaned me, I'll be all set."

"It's yours."

She grinned and after finding the socks, she paid for the items. "Now I'll have to go back and change. Do you want to come—"

"Why not go to Gramps? It's right around the corner, and we can be on our way."

That made sense. "Anyway if I hang around there long enough, you still have my salad."

He nodded with a silly grin on his face. "Unless Gramps ate it."

"If he did—"

"Only teasing." Again, he slipped his arm around her back as they headed down the road.

She loved the closeness and the connection. Chris's manner fell into her category of a perfect date, a perfect man, a perfect... She caught herself and stopped. She was on the Island for a short time, and though she really liked Chris, their relationship hung on the thread of unexpected and short term. Nothing could come of it. Nothing. And yet…

♥

Gramps' head jarred upward when he and Josie came through the door. "Well, look what the cat dragged in."

"Which one of us is the cat, Gramps?"

His grandfather chuckled and shook his head. "You pick, but I vote for the lovely lady on your arm."

Chris rolled his eyes to the delight of his grandfather.

"I bought some new clothes, Harry." She raised the Outfitters bag. "If this man insists on taking me through the snow and wind, I'm choosing to be warmer."

"Good for you, Josie. Even love can't keep everyone warm."

Love? Chris eyed Josie's expression, but she only gave Gramps a wink and didn't insist they were only friends. "You can change in the first bedroom down the hallway on the right." He tilted his head in the direction, and she headed that way.

He watched her as she glanced his way when she went into his room and closed the door. He turned his focus to his grandfather. "What's this thing about love can't keep everyone warm, Gramps?"

"Huh? It's just a saying, Chris. Are you feelin' guilty?"

"No, I'm not feeling guilty, but I don't want to embarrass Josie. We have no commitment, and I've never done anything romantic other than put my arm around her in the cold."

"Good excuse. I used to do that with your grandma."

"Fine. But that doesn't lead to love."

"But it can." A grin crept to his grandfather's mouth. "And when's that first kiss? That can set the deal you know."

"Gramps, you're watching too many romance movies. Please, don't add stress to our friendship."

"So that's what you call it."

"Gramps…" He looked up and spotted Josie in the hallway. "Hey, it looks good. That should keep you warm." He prayed Gramps got the point.

"I hope so, and glad you approve."

She came into the room bundled in her bib pants, and even dressed in that, she looked good to him. Something about Josie touched him in many ways. He eyed his grandfather, curious about what he was thinking.

"Let me put on my snow pants, and then we can be on our way." Chris gave Gramps a look he hoped he understood and hurried to his room.

He left the door open a crack as he tried to listen to his granddad's conversation with Josie. He could imagine him grilling her about her feelings, but all he heard was being happy to have her visit and reminding her of the salad she'd left.

"Gramps, if you'd like the salad, you're welcome to it. It was delicious but I'm going to be out for a while and who knows where we'll be when it's lunch time."

"Thank you." His voice changed, and Chris suspected what Josie would hear next. "I did take a peek at it and it looks delicious. I don't mind eating it if you don't mind."

"Not at all. I hate to waste food, and that was particularly delicious. It would make me happy if you enjoyed it."

"I will, my dear, and I hope you do too…enjoy the ride, I mean."

She chuckled as Chris stepped from his room. He grasped his snow jacket and stepped into the living room. "Sorry to have left you, Josie."

"Not at all. Gramps and I had a nice talk, and I've convinced him to eat the salad since who knows where we'll be at lunch time."

He nodded, figuring that Gramps had already dropped enough hints about the salad to produce the offer. "Good. That way we don't have to rush back."

"You need to take your time, Chris. I'm sure you'll find some very special things to do while you're out there in the woods or stopping to look at the Mackinac Bridge." Gramps gave him a thumbs up. "You never know."

Chris wanted to crawl deep into his snow attire and hide. Heat rose up his chest to his neck, and he feared Gramps and Josie could spot it. He loved his granddad but when Gramps got a plan in his head, it was hard to change it. Somehow he'd decided to play matchmaker. And to be honest, he didn't have to. The more time he spent with Josie, the more he weakened, despite his determination to stay single and focus on Ellie. But then sometimes, he suspected Ellie would love to have a woman in her life to fill the loss of her mom. But who was he to read a child's mind.

"We'd better get moving." He focused on Josie except for a couple of stealthy glimpses at his grandfather, waiting for him to come up with something that would embarrass him, but he didn't.

Josie followed him as they headed out the door, both

waving goodbye to Gramps. Though the sun was shining, the heavy clouds remained, and when the sun slipped behind them, a chill permeated the air. He'd parked the snowmobile close to the back door, and Josie settled in and put her feet on the running boards as he'd instructed the day before. "It's colder today Josie. Are you sure—"

"Positive, Chris. I enjoyed yesterday, and you can show me other parts of the Island and if it's too cold, we can come back."

"That'll work. Just let me know." He loved seeing her eagerness. "Did you notice the surprise I left for you?"

"Surprise?" Her brow wrinkled as she gazed around her but didn't see anything.

He couldn't help but chuckle. "It's right there." He pointed, and she spotted it.

"A thermos. Coffee?"

"No, hot chocolate. I hope that's okay or—"

"Chris, I love hot chocolate. Thanks." She eyed the container. "When did you do that?"

"When you weren't looking."

She chuckled while he slid onto the seat and started the motor. "Okay, hang on."

"I've got my hand on the grips."

"Okay, we're off." He pulled away, eased out to the street and headed up Market Street to Lake View Boulevard. The Mackinac Straits swept past them with a great view of the five-mile suspension bridge connecting the Lower and Upper Peninsulas.

"Gorgeous, Chris. This is a great view."

"Glad you like it." He continued along the road as she oohed and aahed when they passed the Victorian homes facing Lake Michigan. "These homes are called the Grand Ladies. They were built in the 1800s, and as you can see, they are still beautiful."

"Gorgeous. Seeing them up close is special. I've seen them from the ferry ride over from the mainland."

"He revved the motor as he headed up hills and then eased back as they headed down again. By now the street had become Lake Shore Road, and he recalled very well the effort it took on a bicycle. Most tourists got around the Island that way, many pushing the bike up the hills.

When they reached the British Landing, he slowed, then stopped. After he stepped from the vehicle, he helped Josie out. "Be careful of the rocks."

She nodded and sidestepped a couple of large ones. He stood beside her holding her close to his side so she wouldn't trip and fall. That's what he told himself. "This is where the British landed in the War of 1812. They captured Fort Mackinac and took over the whole Island."

"They certainly found a beautiful place to land." She gestured to the view of Lake Huron, St. Ignace and the bridge. "And I can only imagine in warmer weather the water is gorgeous here."

"I suppose that's why weddings are held here." His pulse skipped a beat, and his grandfather's image filled his mind.

"Weddings?" She gazed again at the view and the rocky beach. "I'd hate to trip over some of these rocks and mess up my wedding dress."

A chuckle shot from his throat even though the thought wasn't actually funny. "I'm guessing the wedding party and guests are careful. The persons who handle weddings have chairs they bring here and have rules on decorating. All kinds of things, but it's not uncommon. Although some people choose one of the churches like the Historic Mission Church. It's the oldest church still standing in Michigan."

"I'd like to see that. I'm sure it's lovely."

"It's on the far end of Main St. I think the road is called Huron there. I would guess they're open to the public."

She turned to him, her light brown eyes flickering with golden specks. "Thanks for stopping, Chris. This has been really nice."

To his surprise, she tiptoed up and kissed his cheek while he stood there like a statue, longing to kiss her back.

She gazed at him for a minute until he came out of his dream. "We're about half way once we make a turn up ahead. "I suppose we should go, and we can stop there and have the hot chocolate before it becomes cold chocolate."

She smiled and shook her head. "Either way, I'll like it. It's chocolate, isn't it?" She turned and settled back into the snowmobile and he grinned as he climbed on.

At the turn, he pulled onto the sand, and though a different view, they could still see a few smaller islands off the Upper Peninsula shoreline, the Le Cheneaux area. He pulled out his thermos, and she did the same. When he opened the lid, he was pleased to feel warmth rise from the container.

They sat in silence, sipping the chocolate and gazing onto the blue water. As they finished, snowflakes drifted down, and they leaned back and laughed as the flakes settled on their eyelashes and tongues.

Before he pulled away, the flakes grew into a true snowfall, and he tightened the neck of his jacket and glided away down the east side of the Island. When they neared Arch Rock, he pulled to the side and pointed. "That's what we saw yesterday from above, and here it is from below."

"And look at the steps going up. I like the way we saw it. No stairs, just a great ride on the snowmobile."

He turned and reached for her hand. "You enjoy this?"

"I do, and I enjoy the company." She left her hand in his. "Chris, spending this time with you wasn't part of my plans as you know, but sometimes plans are meant to change, and I really believe that we were destined to meet." A frown darkened her face. "I hope that makes sense. I'm not suggesting anything, but—"

"But I like you too, Josie. I like you a lot, and besides the hot chocolate, I have another surprise."

"Could anything be better than the hot chocolate?" She grinned.

"I think you'll like this. I called Ellie's grandparents and asked them to bring her up here. They said no."

Her jaw dropped. "No? Really? I'm so sorry. I really thought—"

"My parents have agreed, and they'll be arriving next week with Ellie. When they're here, they'll ferry over to see Gramps too, so it's a nice trip."

She leaned forward and threw her arms around his neck. "Chris, I'm so happy for you and for Ellie, and it's great that your parents will visit your granddad too. Harry will be thrilled."

"He will. It will make Christmas perfect, and I'm really grateful that you said what you did. It motivated me."

"What did I say?" Her face tensed, and she surprised him that she'd forgotten."

"You talked about Ellie missing me at Christmas. I would have missed her terribly, and now that I heard her grandparents' attitude, I'm glad I contacted them. Do you know what they said?"

"They said no about bringing her here."

"More than that. They said something about hiring a babysitter to stay with her while they're busy with their Christmas activities." A ragged breath tore through him. "I can't believe they would do that to her."

"I can't either, Chris." She bit her lip, and he noticed her cheek quiver as moisture filled her eyes. "Thank the Lord you called. The poor kid would have been..." She closed her eyes and shook her head. "But your parents are willing to bring her here, and that's wonderful. They must be as nice as you are."

He rested his hand on her shoulder. "Even nicer, Josie. They're great parents."

She raised her hand and pressed it against his cheek. Excitement raced down his limbs, and without thinking, he leaned forward and kissed her lips. Though it was quick, he startled himself. "Josie, I—"

She pressed her index finger against his mouth. "You're wonderful, Chris. Please don't apologize."

He eased back, trying to put the two pieces of her comment together. No matter what she meant, he loved hearing it.

Chapter 4

Josie stood beside Chris as dusk settled on Main Street. People crowded around the Christmas tree, waiting for the lighting and anticipating the joyful feeling of the holidays. Someone at the microphone announced a carol, and the crowd joined in with the words of Deck the Halls. Those who didn't know the words made up their own, but the whole crowd knew the Fa-la-la-la-la, and they sang it with enthusiasm.

Chris slipped his arm around her back, holding her close to his side, and the warmth of his body permeated her insulated clothing. The sensation surprised her, and her smile deepened as the crowd joined in the next song, O Come All Ye Faithful.

As they sang the dusk faded into darkness, but the Christmas lights on the building cut the night with shafts of color that splayed on the snow that had accumulated during the afternoon. Children congregated close to the front, and Chris pointed and winked. "They all want to be the one chosen to hit the switch and bring life to the Christmas tree. They select one child every year with the honor."

"If I were a kid, I'd be there too. Everyone likes to be chosen." The words knotted as they left her, thinking back to times in her youth when her two older sisters seemed to have everything. She got the leftovers, but then most kids probably felt that way.

Today she could only think about both sisters, now divorced, one living alone and the other with a child. That was the last thing in the world she wanted. Thoughts of marriage had exited her mind years earlier as she watched her sister's suffer through the agony of loss and change. It wasn't for her. Not at all.

Yet, she stood beside Chris with his warmth surrounding her, his smile rousing her smile, and his kindness meaning the world to her. Had her sisters felt that way once? Love could sometimes blind people from the truth. How could she ever trust herself to see what was real rather than a fantasy, like a child's fairytale story?

Chris had turned toward her, and she realized she'd been too quiet. She managed a grin and leaned her head on his shoulder, hoping it would ease his concern. A moment later, the big announcement came, and the child chosen let out a happy yell. The crowd shifted closer, and the count began. Three. Two. One. The lights burst into colors with a silver star glowing at the top.

Those who lived there seemed to know what was next. They quieted and the words of Silent Night filled the night. At the end of the song, the sound of sleigh bells tinkled off in the distance, but they grew louder, and soon a large hay wagon made its way to the crowd.

Chris leaned closer to her ear. "This is another

tradition."

"Every year?"

"Every year. Would you like to go?"

She eyed the wagon and grinned. "I haven't been on a hayride since I was a teenager."

He gave her a hug. "Then it's time you go again. Let's get on before we can't find a spot." He took her arms and steered her toward the wagon as others were climbing on. He gave her a push upward, and then he hoisted himself beside her.

She felt a kind of camaraderie that evaded her more often than not, but today the fun of having Chris beside her, helping her on and holding her close gave her an amazing feeling. The lights from the tree added an aura of expectation like opening a book by a favorite author and knowing it would be wonderful. So many things with Chris, even simple things, became a fantastic experience.

Some of the crowd headed toward their homes and some to the fire barn or to the community hall where Chris explained they were holding a rummage sale. Others stood and watched as the horses lumbered away from the crowd. The sway of the wagon created a gentle rhythm as they headed up Main Street, and she leaned back on her elbows with Chris leaning on his as he faced her.

"You're a beautiful woman, Josie."

"It's the Christmas lights not me." She smiled, but her dancing heart admitted more than she wanted to feel. "Nights like this are almost a fairytale. The carols, the sense of community, the lights spreading across the snow and touching people's skin." She drew in a breath. "And then a hayride heading for a mystic forest."

"Probably not. They usually head up Cadette." He gave her the sweetest smile she'd ever seen.

Someone behind them began to sing again, and others joined in with Jingle Bells, fitting to the sounds of the horse bells tinkling along as they tugged the wagon.

"Come here." Chris sat up and beckoned her into his arms.

She shifted around and pressed her back against his chest while his arms embraced her, and his breathing whispered against her cheek. Others seemed to ignore them, and she longed to have the nerve to turn around and kiss him, the kind of kiss that she'd read about in novels but never experienced.

Chris seemed to have the same idea since he maneuvered closer and kissed her cheek before pressing his cheek to hers. He wore a fragrance that she'd never smelled. Perhaps she'd never been close enough to take in the scent. It reminded her of pine trees and a touch of musk. An earthy aroma that aroused her senses.

"It's too bad Ellie couldn't be here with us." She turned to look into his eyes, and his look sent her heart skipping.

"She would love it, but we can take her on a carriage ride. They still have taxi service in the winter, and we could go someplace with her for dinner, maybe."

"That would be fun. Not quite a hayride but maybe even better."

"Josie, I'm so glad your jacket fell off your chair."

His unexpected comment made her laugh. "I am too, Chris. I would have already left for home by now and missed all these wonderful tradition, but most of all..." She looked at his expression and her pulse waltzed through her. "Most of all, I met you. You are special." She gasped for air. "This vacation offered me far more than I ever anticipated. Carol and I would have shopped and tried to see a little of the Island, and with you, I'm living the Island."

He gazed at her with a depth that swept through her heart. "And you gave me life too, Josie. I was here for Gramps, and since I met you, I'm also here for us."

Us. Not you. Not me. But us. "That has a lovely sound, Chris."

"It does. I never imagined saying that to anyone, but you're different, and I love the difference."

"Our friendship is different."

They sat in silence, listening to a few people singing carols and others whispering in the darkness. The wagon wove through a bit of woods and soon returned to the city. They lumbered down Market Street and paused outside the Fire Barn. "Anyone ready for the rummage sale?"

She looked at Chris, and he shrugged. "Only if you want to look."

"Not really."

"We can get off here and head back, if you'd like. Your place is up ahead, or if you want to go to Gramps, we can do that, and I'll bring you back later."

She nodded. "Gramps."

His face blossomed like a flower. "Good." He slipped down from the wagon, grasped her by the waist and lifted her down beside him, like a feather. "Thank you, kind sir."

He gave a low sweeping bow. "It was my pleasure."

He wrapped her hand in his, and they headed down Market Street while her feet seemed to be gliding about the snowy sidewalk. The man did work magic.

♥

Chris stood in the moonlight as snow drifted past while he waited for the light to turn on in Josie's room at the Cottage Inn. They'd had a wonderful night together, except he'd longed to kiss her, a real kiss that neither would forget, but he'd backed down. Though he cared a lot for Josie, he'd made a decision to never marry. When he'd agreed to be a guardian to his brother Gary's daughter, he never expected to be taken up on it. Gary and Mindy's deaths had knocked him off his foundation, and with Ellie in his life, he had no desire to muddle her life anymore than she'd already had to experience.

As much as he thought of Josie, he couldn't guarantee that she felt the same or that when they left Mackinac Island their feelings would stay as strong as his had grown. Giving Ellie the experience of someone else in her life who might walk away was beyond his ability to take a chance. And yet part of him desired her. He would have taken a chance. Josie made him confident and comfortable. She caused him to laugh and get excited about everyday things. Even preparing a meal had become a new adventure.

Flakes caught on his lashes and he brushed them away. As he looked up, he spotted Josie in the window, watching him. She raised her hand, and as silly as it seemed, his heart skipped. A wave from Josie could do that. He waved back and then turned toward his granddad's house.

The air had grown nippier, and he took longer

strides, passing the darkened shops along the way, and when he turned onto French Lane, relief washed through him. Warmth and Gramps. A place he could think and plan for Ellie's visit. When he told Josie he was grateful she'd encouraged him to bring Ellie there, he meant it. He would never have forgiven himself later when he learned what Mindy's parents had planned for Ellie's Christmas. That was something he didn't think he could forgive.

"Look who's back."

Gramps voice reached him before he saw him. "It's getting really nippy out there, Gramps."

"You said it was getting colder when you were here earlier." He motioned toward the sofa. "How did the celebration go?"

"Before the tree lighting we sang carols, then afterward, we went on the hayride."

"And that's it?"

Chris sank onto the sofa. "What does that mean?"

"How about the kiss?"

"Gramps, what's gotten into you?"

His granddad guffawed and slapped his leg. "That's my question to you. You have this lovely young woman here. You're hanging out together everyday. She's perfect for you. Not just good-lookin' but a very nice woman, and yet you're draggin' your feet."

"My feet are fine. And you didn't ask about my feet. You wanted to know if I kissed her, and yes, I did."

"Now you're talkin.' That can move things along a little faster."

"I kissed her on the cheek, Gramps, and I'm moving as fast as I care to."

Gramps raised both hands and pressed his face into them. "Whose grandson are you?"

"Come on, Gramps. For me, that was progress."

"Progress? So is a turtle climbing a mountain. You're going to lose her, Chris, and—"

"Gramps." He couldn't sit anymore and listen. He rose and strutted toward his granddad. "Look, I'm moving as fast as I want, and I'm not sure I'm trying to make progress. I have Ellie, and she needs me...needs my full attention. If Josie were in my life, it could cause problems, and I don't want to do that to Ellie. She's been through enough."

Gramps tossed back his head and closed his eyes. "Chris, first, you need to remember that one day Ellie will want and need a mom. You also have a good chance once she's here to test her reaction to Josie. See what happens, but my bet is that she'll love her just like I do...and you do. I'm not blind. You're a different man since Josie came into your life. You're alive. Finally.

"What do you mean I'm alive? Was I dead before she came? I have things to do, things to take care of, and I can't be a Casanova, Gramps. I've never been one, and I don't plan to be."

"Good. I didn't expect you to be that. But you need to give love a chance, Chris. I see you look into her eyes, and your face lights up. You glow like—"

"We've only known each other three weeks. Not even that. Did you fall in love with Grandma in three weeks?"

"Nope, it probably took three days. I knew then that she was special. She made me feel special, and yet she knew I wasn't perfect. We had a great relationship, Chris, and it only took days to realize it."

"I guess I'm slower than that." He turned his back and headed toward the hallway. "I'm going to bed Gramps. I'm tired." He didn't wait for a response, but in his heart, he sensed his grandfather was correct. When he met Josie, he knew right away that she was amazing. She captured him as fast as a bear trap. Yet, he wanted to deny it. Hearing Gramps, he realized he'd failed an opportunity to test Ellie's ability to share. Even worse, he'd cheated his own ability to test himself.

♥

Chris met Josie after breakfast. She suggested they go to Main Street and Christmas shop, and he was sure she had Ellie in mind. The auction started after lunch at two o'clock at the Community Hall close to the Cottage Inn, so it would be convenient to drop off her packages.

The sun, backed by a clear blue sky, sent down warm rays, and being outside today seemed pleasurable. When he arrived at Cottage Inn, Josie stepped out in pants, a bulky sweater with her regular jacket. No insulated pants and coats needed today.

He held her hand as they walked along Market to Astor, and they both grinned when they passed Mustang Lounge, the place they'd met. She remained quiet, and yet she seemed relaxed. He assumed she'd slept well, and he wished he had. "Where should we head?"

"We can walk and see what we discover."

"Got it." They walked side by side and turned on Main Street. I want to get something for Ellie. I thought of books or maybe a stuffed animal. What do you think?"

"She likes stuffed toys, but she loves books. There's

a toy store in town so we can look there." He squeezed her hand and her face brightened.

"I'm surprised how excited I am that Ellie is going to be here. Children add something to Christmas. I think they remind me of my childhood and how excited I was to see gifts under the tree, and to go to church with all the decorations and candles. It was another fairytale for me."

"Did you ever think that you might be a fairytale prince hiding out the real world?"

She punched his arm. "Silly. I know I am."

He released her hand and shifted his arm around her waist. "You're my princess, Josie."

"That's what Ellie needs. A tiara."

He chuckled at her imagination, and yet he enjoyed the fairytale idea too. "Perhaps I'm your princess charming, and I'll come out of hiding once you put on your tiara."

She shook her head. "I think we're both off the deep end now. We should save this for Ellie."

"We will." He looked up and spotted a couple of shops that were open. "Here we are." He pointed to the Open sign. When she smiled, he couldn't shift his eyes from her lips. Maybe Gramps was right. A real kiss could validate his feelings. Once Ellie was there, sneaking a kiss might be more complicated. He needed to act soon. Make a plan.

Or was a kiss impromptu, happening at the exact time it was meant to be?

♥

With her arms full, Josie returned to the Cottage Inn. Though she thought about attending the auction, she decided to give Chris a break. He'd followed her from store to store that they found open, while she picked up little trinkets and gifts for Christmas. She bought her Cottage Inn hostess, a pretty vase. She'd noticed Rose's décor selections, and the vase was exactly right for her. She even picked up a scarf for Chris's mother and a more manly one for his father. Hopefully they would like them or at least appreciate her effort.

Gramps was easy. He liked everything, and she found a warm plaid shirt that Chris thought he would like. She'd even sneaked a pair of black leather gloves for Chris into her purchases. Looking for gifts for Ellie was the most fun. A plush, fluffy kitten that purred. What child wouldn't love that?

And she couldn't resist a book filled with well-known fairytales with bright pictures and stories of love and being saved by prince charming. Chris agreed that it was a great choice, and as she looked into his eyes, her chest tightened as her imagination soared. Could he be her very own prince charming? But when she gave it more thought, her imagination faded to reality. No prince charmings for her. Never. They were all fantasy.

After putting the packages away in her closet, she returned to the Cottage Inn lounge where Rose always set a plate full of homemade cookies and a carafe of coffee. She selected a cookie, poured a cup of brew and settled into an easy chair, her mind drifting back to her unexpected island revision of plans.

"Back so early?"

Josie lifted her head and grinned at Rose. "I'm giving my poor tour guide a break. He's been so great, and I don't want to wear him out."

"Your tour guide?" Rose cocked her head while

confusion twisted her face.

"Chris. He's such a nice man and offered to show me the island when he learned that Carol couldn't make it."

"And that's all he is? A tour guide?"

Though she got Rose's point, she couldn't deal with explaining it. She didn't understand it herself.

"I guess we're becoming casual friends." Why had she added casual? The word seemed inappropriate and unneeded. And Rose didn't believe it anyway from her expression.

"Casual friend. Is that what they call it now?"

Josie pressed her lips together to stop herself from denying the truth. "I will admit that I'm having fun, and he seems to be enjoying himself, too, but then he might be a good actor."

"I don't think so, Josie. I've watched him with you when he stops by. I think he cares a great deal about you, and now that he's bringing Ellie here, and with your encouragement, I'm sure he's expecting you to join in the fun of entertaining the little girl. You know she's been without a mother for a couple of years, and though those memories are probably faint, she sees other children with a female in their lives, and I'm guessing a woman's attention is something she needs."

A ragged breath escaped before Josie could monitor it. "That's a big responsibility for someone who doesn't have a child."

"But mothering often comes natural to women, and even men. Look at Chris. He's taken over the father role and apparently doing a good job." She held up her hand. "This really isn't my business, Josie, and I'm just repeating things that you've told me so I'm not an authority, but if I heard you correctly, I think I'm right."

Josie's head spun with the details Rose had sent her way, and yes, Rose had told the story correctly, although she'd added a few assumptions that Josie wasn't sure were accurate. It seemed as if Rose knew her better than she knew herself. Did she have a talent with children? She'd had very little experience with them, not even with Carol's son, Jacob, since they lived so far away.

"I suppose time will tell. I'm not going to walk away from him now. I encouraged him to bring Ellie here, and he let me know that he'd made a bad decision by not including her from the beginning, but then he knew his granddad needed help, and he didn't know how much time that would take." Why was she defending Chris and her big mouth.

"You're right, Josie. Time will tell, and I think you'll be pleased."

"Thanks for the vote of confidence." She took a sip of her coffee, hoping to end the conversation.

"Are you doing anything tonight?"

"Not much. We're going to have dinner at Chris's granddad's. I'm not sure if they're ordering in or if someone is cooking. I hope it's not me."

Rose chuckled. "It'll be an adventure."

"That's what I'm afraid of." She laughed, too. "These are great cookies. You have some wonderful recipes."

"Thanks. I didn't think of myself as a cook until I opened the bed and breakfast. When I made that commitment, I didn't have an option. I guess it proves that when we're determined, we can learn new things and be a success."

"You know, Rose, maybe I can learn from that too."

"I'm sure you can. Wait until Ellie gets here—and that's soon—you'll be surprised what you can do."

"I hope so." She ate the end of the cookie and washed it down with the now cool coffee. "I'd better decide what I'll wear tonight. Knowing Chris, we may be on the snowmobile again."

"Or maybe you'll be sitting on the porch, watching the sun sink below the horizon as the amazing sweep of stars appear in the sky."

Josie leaned back, the picture filling her mind. "I like that idea. There's something about the stars that touch the imagination."

"There is. It's the mystery and beauty of God's handiwork. Have a great evening." Rose stood a moment before turning around and heading back to the private rooms.

Chapter 5

Chris stood at the ferry dock and checked his watch. Ellie was to arrive with his parents, but their ferry hadn't docked yet, and he assumed something happened to make them late. He wished they had sent him a text or called so he could stop worrying. He glanced over his shoulder, unable to understand why Josie hadn't come with him. She'd said that Ellie would be excited to see him, and she didn't want to dampen the occasion.

Dampen the occasion? He didn't understand what that meant. How could she ruin Ellie's arrival or his parents? He'd looked forward to her meeting all of them. He leaned his shoulder against the door frame leading onto the ferry dock and watched the next arrival head toward him across the straits from Mackinaw City.

His pulse skipped anticipating Ellie's sweet smile as she ran to him, calling "Daddy Chris." She needed a daddy, but he hadn't wanted to take her real father's place. And yet that's what he'd promised to do when Gary and Mindy had asked him to be guardian. A breath rattled from him, and he closed his eyes, reliving the day when he received the horrible news that they had both been killed in the car accident.

Ellie had been only two, but she knew something was wrong. She cried for her mother and father until the family could no longer bear it. And yet they did. Before her third birthday, he recalled Ellie looking at him one day and said, "Bye, bye. They went to heaven."

Tears blurred his eyes, and yet he had to hide the painful memories and smile in agreement. She sometimes asked if they were watching her, and he always said yes. He knew they were so proud of her. By her fourth birthday, Ellie continued to think of them, but she mentioned Gary and Mindy in a more positive way. She would say, "Mommy is happy that I'm helping." His throat knotted even without speaking. Yes, her mommy was very happy, and he believed it as much as Ellie did.

His memory drifted as he watched the ferry boat pull into the slip. A dockhand grabbed the rope and tied the vessel to the mooring. People crowded down the steps from the upper deck, while others pushed their way along the lower level toward the gangplank.

He studied the crowd, hoping to spot his parents if not Ellie. This trip was her first, and he knew she would be excited to tell him about crossing the Straits. Focused on the crowd heading down the dock, he jerked when a hand touched his arm, and he spun around and faltered. "Josie. I thought—"

"The more I weighed my decision the dumber it became, Chris. I had looked forward to meeting your family, and I saw the expression on your face when I told you I wasn't going to go to the dock with you. And—"

"And you're here. That's what's important. You've made me happy." He slipped his arm around her waist and drew her closer as his focus shifted to the passengers exiting the ferry. "There they are." He pointed toward the crowd. "Dad's carrying Ellie on his shoulders."

Josie rose on tiptoes. "I think I see him. Does she have hair the color of yours?"

"I guess. It's dark brown with some lighter highlights in the sun."

"That's her, then."

She grinned at him, and his heart lifted. He drew her closer and waved. Ellie spotted him because she started wiggling and waving, and he watched his dad try to dodge her wild arm movements as he lowered her to the dock.

When they reached him, he opened his arms to Ellie and gave her a hug. Her small frame always melted his heart when she cuddled with him in the morning or sometimes as he carried her to bed after she'd fallen asleep.

"Dad. Mom. This is Joselyn Ryan. She lives in the Detroit area and came up to spend time with a friend, but her friend ended up not making it. It's a long story."

"Nice to meet you, Joselyn." His father extended his hand, and his mother followed.

"Thanks. I already know you're good people. Anyone who raised Chris has to be. He's a very kind man, and I'm sure you'll hear the story about my messed up plans and how he made my trip worthwhile."

"Mom, don't listen to her. She's prejudice."

His mother shook her head with a grin. "So am I. And I agree with her. Your dad and I did a good job raising you if I do say so myself. I'll have to tell Joselyn about some of your pranks when you were a kid."

"Please call me Josie, Mrs. Banks. That's what my friends do."

"Okay, Josie and you can call me Lizzie, and Mr. Banks is Brian."

"I've looked forward to meeting you." She turned toward Ellie who was clinging to Chris. "And I've wanted to meet Ellie. I heard very nice things about her."

Ellie glanced her way and whispered something to Chris. He chuckled. "Ellie wants to know if I told you the truth."

Josie shrugged. "I think he did, Ellie, and from what I see today, I think he's right. He said you're his favorite four-year-old in the whole world."

Ellie almost whip-lashed her neck, turning to face him. "You did, Daddy Chris?"

He hadn't said that exactly, but Josie knew enough that she had made the perfect guess. "I sure did."

Ellie wrapped her arms tighter around him. "I love you."

"I love you to the planets and back, Ellie."

"It's the moon." Ellie gave him a silly look. "You said it wrong."

"No I didn't. The planets are farther than the moon so that means I love even more than the moon and back."

Her face brightened as she giggled.

"We'd better be on our way. We're blocking the path of these eager people to get to their hotels."

He lowered Ellie to the ground but continued to

hold her hand until he spotted the luggage. She shifted her gaze to Josie once in a while as if not sure if she should get too close.

Chris motioned to the baggage piled in the ferry building. "Mom, will you take her hand so I can help with the luggage?"

His mom scooted between them and drew Ellie's hand in hers. "We'll meet you out on the sidewalk."

Josie joined Lizzie and Ellie working their way through the crowd to wait, and when Chris stepped onto the sidewalk, pulling a large suitcase, he saw them standing away from the entrance. "Mom, we're close to Gramps. Can you walk?"

"Me? Certainly. Dad and I try to get a walk in most days when the weather is good."

"Great. Josie, come with us. Gramps decided to cook, if you can believe it. He made chili soup. Whatever it is, it smelled good when I left the house."

His Dad caught up with them, pulling two small overnight bags. "I'm starving so I'm glad to hear there's food."

"Brian, you have enough fat on your bones to live a long time without food." His mom shook her finger at him.

His dad gave him a wink and didn't comment. In his eyes, his dad looked pretty good. In fact, he'd thought he'd lost weight.

They crossed the street in front of Lake View Hotel and rounded the corner to French Lane. His parents had been there before, but a few years had passed. Yet, he was confident they would recognize Gramps's house. They hurried up the porch, and Gramps opened the door as if he'd been standing guard waiting for them to arrive. "Brian. Lizzie. So good to see you." He opened his arms and gave them both a hug, and then he bent down and pulled something from his pocket. "And Ellie, I have something for you." Gramps handed her a lollipop, and she took it, but looked at him for approval.

Chris grinned. "You can eat it after lunch, Ellie. Let's save it."

She eyed the sucker and then gave in and handed it to him. "Thank you, Grandpa."

Chris tousled her hair "Did you know, Ellie, that this is your Great Grandpa."

She gave him a blank look as his eyebrows pinched together. "What's a Great Grandpa?"

Gramps touched his chest. "I'm great, because your Grandpa…" He pointed to Brian. "Is my son. I'm his father, so that makes me Great."

She frowned and then grinned. "Is Grandma great too."

Gramps slapped his knee. "She sure is, but not in the same way. She's great because she puts up with all of us and loves us."

Ellie gave her a big grin. "Grandma, you're great too." She shifted away from him and hurried to her side, then hugged her around the legs.

"Thank you, Ellie. I think everyone standing here is pretty great."

"Me too." Ellie eyed Josie a moment and then appeared to dismiss her and skipped around the room until she stopped near the kitchen door. "Do we get to eat?"

"We sure do." Gramps joined her, and they hurried into the kitchen.

His parents headed that way too, but he stayed and

caught Josie's hand while they were alone. "What do you think?"

"I think I'm hungry." She grinned, and it warmed him.

"The soup does smell good. I didn't realize Gramps was a good cook, but I suppose he had to learn to be when Grandma died."

"We have to learn all through our lives. I was talking with Rose about that yesterday."

"I trust you're right." He gave a quick nod.

"Chris."

The tone of her voice caught his interest. "Is something wrong?"

"No. Not at all." She pressed her hand against his arm. "I wondered if you realize how much Ellie looks like you."

"Ellie?"

"Yes, she not only has your hair color but also your eyes, both color and shape, and even her mouth and the hint of a dimple. She could easily be your own child."

Her comment unbalanced him for a moment. He wished she were his child at times, but she wasn't, and yet he often felt as if she were. "Gary and I did have similar features. He was a little shorter and I think his face was rounder than mine—more like Mom's I guess—but to be honest, I feel as if I'm her father sometimes."

"She's darling. So full of love and a bit of shyness too. I love the way she does something or says something and then looks around for approval before she finishes."

"I hadn't really noticed that, but now that you say it, you're right. She's tentative at times, and maybe that happened from losing her parents. I often wonder if she ever thinks she did something to make that happen. Still she was so young, I don't think that was the case."

"But she's smart, Chris, and who knows what happened in that young mind of hers. I'm new eyes here. If I notice anything I'll let you know."

"Thanks. I hoped to get some feedback from you. The situation still hurts me. Not that I promised to raise her, but that Gary and Mindy aren't here to love her and see her become a young lady. She is a sweet little girl."

"She's darling, and I understand what you're saying. It's heartbreaking."

"Hey, Lovebirds."

They both did a double take as Gramps' voice sailed into the living room. Chris heard his parents laugh while Josie shook her head. "I suppose we'd better go in and eat, or we'll never hear the last of it."

"Right."

He slipped his hand in hers and headed to the kitchen, but before they entered, he dropped his arm to avoid any more comments. Gramps had a great knack for embarrassing him.

♥

Josie placed her spoon on the saucer and leaned back. After Harry's delicious chili, she'd turned into a balloon with too much air that it was ready to burst. "Your chili was wonderful, Harry. Thanks for inviting me."

Ellie eyed her a moment, and as if she'd become a mimic. She placed her spoon on the plate and leaned back, seeming to check to make sure she'd done it right. "The chili was wonderful, Grandpa." Her eyes widened. "No. It's Great Grandpa."

Chris's father let out a chuckle. "Grandpa can get a bit confusing. Right, Ellie? You have two of us here. Let's see how we can fix it."

He eyed Chris a moment. "You call Harry Gramps, right?"

"I sure do."

"Ellie, you can call your Great Granddad Gramps, and me Grandpa. How's that?"

Her brow furrowed as if she'd been asked to make a major life decision. Josie had pressed her lips together, he suspected, to avoid a grin. Finally, Ellie nodded. "Okay, Grandpa, and thank you for the good dinner, Gramps."

"You're welcome, Angel."

She tilted her head and eyed him. "My mom is an angel, Gramps."

He flinched and appeared to try to cover his bad choice of words. "She is, Ellie, but you can be an angel on earth. It'll be good practice."

"Okay." A sweet grin ended her more serious expression.

Jumping in to change the subject, Chris pointed to the window. "Ellie, do you see what's happening outside?"

She turned as her eyes widened. "It's snowing." She clapped her hands and darted from the table to the view outside. "Can we play in it, Daddy Chris?"

He gave Josie a sidelong look. "What do you say?"

"I say okay, but I'll need to change clothes."

"Oh. Oh." Ellie's frown returned. "Do I have a warm coat?"

Chris's mom nodded. "I put your snow clothes in the bottom of your luggage. I'll help you find it."

"Okay." She hurried from the window and headed for the hallway.

"Ellie." Chris stood and beckoned to her. "We just finished eating so let's help Gramps get the kitchen cleaned up and rest our tummies, okay? Then we can go out, and....there'll be more snow."

That made Ellie's eyes widen even more. "I'll help." She grabbed her chili bowl and hurried to the counter top near the sink. Everyone tittered, but tried to mute it so Ellie didn't hear them.

Josie rose, piled the plates and a few bowls and joined Ellie at the sink. The child had pulled a chair up and was trying to rinse the dishes, but more water had gotten on her and the floor than on the dishes.

"Let me help you. Okay?"

Ellie gazed at her a moment before she agreed.

"You keep rinsing, Ellie, and I'll put the dishes in the dishwasher. How's that?"

"Okay. Cuz I can't put 'em in good enough. That's what Grandma says."

She wondered if it was Chris's mom who made that comment or the other grandmother. She guessed it was Mindy's mother. "One day when we have lots of time, I'll show you how to put them in. Would you like that?"

Her head wagged like the tail of a happy dog. "Then I can do it right."

"I'm sure you will be able to. You're a smart girl. I can see that."

"You can?" A tiny grin curved her lips.

"I sure can." She reached over and gave her a quick hug. As Josie pulled away, she sensed someone stood behind her. She turned seeing Chris holding more dishes in his hands and watching them. The others apparently had gone to the living room.

"If you give those to the young lady at the sink, she'll rinse them while I load them into the dishwasher."

"Ah." He moved closer and did as she said. "You have a system going, I see."

"Daddy Chris, Josie and I have a system."

He tousled her hair and then leaned over and kissed her cheek. "You are both very kind ladies."

"But I'm not a lady yet."

"Soon. You're growing up fast, Ellie."

She giggled and went back to her work. But Chris stood behind Ellie while his eyes scanned Josie's. "Do you want to go back to the Inn and get ready? I can finish the loading."

Josie shrugged. "I suppose I should." He rested his hand on her arm and gave it a squeeze. "Thanks for..."

She nodded. "It's fun."

Ellie spun around and surprised her. "Do you think putting dishes in there is fun?"

"No, but I think doing them with you is fun."

Ellie's eyes widened again. "You do. Why?"

"Because you're special."

She shifted her gaze to Chris. "Am I special?"

"As special as they get, Ellie my love." Chris tousled her hair.

She skipped around the kitchen lilting "I'm special" as if it were a song. Chris clamped his jaw, she assumed, to control a laugh, and as Ellie swept past him, he scooped her into his arms and joined her silly song. "You're special. You're special."

"Hold on here."

They all spun around to find Gramps standing in the

kitchen doorway. "You should let all of us sing." He gave a wink. "Let me finish this job while you get ready to go out. Once the sun goes down, it'll get nippy. Have fun while the sun shines."

Chris held up his hand. "I think it's 'Make hay while the sun shines.'"

As soon as the words flew into the air, Josie could see that he wished he hadn't. And she knew why."

Gramps guffawed and slapped his knee. "You can call it whatever you want, Chris. But you get my meaning." He slapped his leg again and headed for the sink. "Ellie girl, you need to get ready too. Grandma is waiting for you."

"Okay." She held on to the chair back and lowered herself to the ground before darting off. "Grandma, I need to get ready."

Chris gave her a wink. "I guess we'd better make that hay or it'll be too cold."

She shook her head at his silliness and headed toward the living room to get her coat and walk back to Cottage Inn.

Chapter 6

Chris held Ellie's hand as they headed toward Cottage Inn. Still a block away, he spotted Josie hurrying toward them. She pointed behind her, and he looked past her to see what she was indicating. Finally, he caught on. Marquette Park butted up to Fort Mackinac and offered a wide expanse of grass now covered with snow.

He signaled for Josie to wait while he and Ellie picked up pace and met her just before Astor Street. "Let's keep going, and we'll get to the park. I think that's what you meant."

"It is. I thought it might be a fun place to play."

Ellie heard the key word and skipped ahead. "Let's play." As she twirled around, her foot slipped and down she went. He hurried ahead and pulled her up before her tears flowed, but instead she was laughing. "I'm silly. Right, Daddy Chris."

"You sure are." He collected her hand in his, and Josie took the other side. At first, Ellie eyed her hand in hers, but in a minute, she appeared to accept it and saw it as a way to have more fun. Every few minutes, Ellie lifted her feet, and they would swing her forward, but with the slippery snow, he feared one of them would end up falling. Yet when they got to Fort Street, he knew they were safe. Once they crossed the road, they were in the park.

As soon as they had reached the center, he bent down and grasped a handful of snow and formed it into a ball. "Ellie. Look here."

She spun around, and he flung the soft snowball her way and it hit her chest. Though she looked surprised, she finally laughed and grabbed a gob of her own. Her snowball wasn't as successful, but he put on a show to make her think she'd done a good job, and Josie joined in.

When another family arrived and started a snowman, Ellie wanted to make one too. Seeing her excitement, his aroused too. They rolled a large ball of snow for the base, and then worked at adding the smaller ball and finally the head. With no hat or carrot, they had to be creative. Ellie ran toward the fort where she saw the green bushes and he suspected that they could find twigs and sticks that might serve as arms and a nose for the snowman.

Josie gave them a wave. "Look what I have." She slid to their side, holding two medium sized stones to use as eyes, and a few smaller ones to shape a mouth. Ellie appeared with a piece of twig which she declared the nose, and he had found two longer sticks for the arms. When they finished the snowman, he pulled out his cell phone and hit the camera icon. With Josie on one side and Ellie nestled on the other, he took their photo.

The girls rushed forward, gazing at the screen as they laughed. But Ellie tugged at his jacket. "Daddy Chris, we want you in the picture too."

"Sweetie, there's no one to take our picture and a selfie won't work. The picture wouldn't get all of us in."

"Why?" Her sweet face, wrinkled with her displeasure.

"Because my arms aren't long enough."

She eyed his arm as he stretched it out in front of them, hoping she'd accept his answer.

"Can I help you?" A man passing by approached them, and he realized he was with the family making the other snowman. "Would you like me to take the photo?"

Chris grinned and handed him his cell phone. "Sure. Do you know how to—"

"I do. It's like mine." He backed up while the three of them cuddled around the snowman."

He took more than one shot and handed back the phone. "I think I got a good one."

"Thanks so much." He glanced down and hit the gallery button. The pictures opened, and he swept through the three the man took while Ellie tugged at his jacket. "I want to see too." Josie stepped beside him and he handed her the phone and hoisted Ellie onto his hip. As he gazed at the photographs, his heart squeezed, seeing the cozy scene of three happy people and a goofy looking snowman. And yet, the photo touched his heart with Josie's gorgeous smile, Ellie's shining face and his look of contentment as if they were a real family.

He lowered Ellie to the snowy ground. She had

gotten her wish, and he sensed a wish of his own pushing its way into his chest.

"It's time to go back, I suspect." He glanced at his watch and looked at the horizon. Though the sun was still midway in the sky, the cooler air zipped through his jacket and into his bones.

"Not yet." Ellie tilted her head and looked at him and then Josie. "I think Josie wants to play more."

Josie arched an eyebrow. "I was thinking that maybe—"

Before she finished her sentence, Ellie had flung herself into a clean patch of snow and spread her legs and arms back and forth making a snow angel. He eyed Josie, and she gave a faint shrug which is how he felt. "Ellie, now you're going to freeze."

"No. I'm making an angel for Mommy and Daddy." She gazed up at him before shifting her eyes to Josie. "See." She eased herself up and stepped away from the perfect angel shape embedded in the white powder.

"It's beautiful, Ellie." Josie stepped beside her and gave her a hug. "Your Mom and Dad will love it."

"See, Daddy Chris. Josie says they can see my angel."

He nearly rolled his eyes but managed to contain the urge. "If Josie says it, then they do see it."

Ellie slipped her hand into Josie's. "Cuz we're girls, and we understand."

He cringed at her wisdom. So often he noticed that a woman would handle a problem in a different way or have the right thing to say that he didn't. Men saw the world differently sometimes. Women saw it with emotion but also with commonsense. Somehow women had a storehouse of words and ideas that he didn't have.

Ellie needed a mom, and even though he'd promised to be her guardian, he could still do that but have Ellie live with his mom and dad if they were willing or... His chest tightened as thoughts tumbled from his mind. He'd promised his brother and wife, and the job remained his. How could he even think of giving her to someone else? He adored the little girl. She brightened his life, and he owed it to her and his brother to stay true to his promise.

Anyway, even the thought of Ellie out of his life broke his heart. What had he been thinking?

♥

Josie sat at the breakfast table, sipping coffee, her mind piled with thought. Today, Chris's parents were heading back home, and she was supposed to go with them to the ferry dock. But she paused, concerned about where things were going. Instead, it might be a good time to make an excuse and skip the event. The family needed privacy. Though she'd become highly involved with Chris and even his family while they were here, she needed to step out of the picture for the day.

"You look like you're carrying the weight of the world." Rose appeared behind her with the coffee carafe." She didn't ask but filled her cup.

"Lots of things on my mind, Rose, but I don't need to burden you."

"No burden. Are you unhappy? I thought you were enjoying your time with Chris and with the little girl. Ellie? Is that it?"

"Yes, Ellie. She's a dear, but I'm observing things, and I guess I'm over-thinking."

"Over-thinking?"

"I'm not sure. She's a vibrant child, but at times I sense she needs more attention. She's been a good child. Very quiet sometimes, but other times, much more open."

Rose pulled up the empty chair at her table and sat. "Has something in particular caused you to be concerned?"

"I suppose it happened yesterday when she made a snow angel. She made reference to her parents. You know they're deceased. Her behavior made me ask myself questions. Does Chris talk to her about her parents? They died when she was two, and I'm guessing that her memory would most likely be faded to only a shadow." She paused and shook her head. "Or maybe no shadow at all. Her references to them might be based solely on what she'd heard or learned since she'd become old enough to hang on to information. And yet..." A stream of air left her lungs. "I don't know Rose, and it's really not my business."

"You care about her, Josie. And you care about Chris. You know, it's obvious. It's natural to be concerned or to wonder.

"But, Rose, really, who am I to try and solve the child's problems. Chris has proven to me that he's a good guardian, even more like a father. He dotes on her, and his love can't be questioned." Her heart skipped. "But then Ellie is easy to love." The realization caught in her throat.

Rose reached over and patted her arm. "And you realize that you love the little girl."

She again blew air from her lungs. "Rose, I'm afraid you're right. But I'll be leaving for home soon, and Chris and Ellie will be too. The worst thing I could do would be to get too involved with them. We live in two separate worlds and..." She swallowed her admission that she had no interest in commitment or marriage.

"Those issues can be fixed, Josie. If you truly care and I sense you do, as well as caring for Chris. I think he cares about you, so logistics are fixable. Don't give up something worthwhile because of those things.

"I just think I'm adding a bump to the road?"

"Whose road?"

Josie lifted her shoulders and dropped them. "I don't know." She stared at the tablecloth while her mind reeled. "I'm confused, I guess."

"Then stop thinking and start feeling. I think that's—"

Her cell phone rang, interrupting Rose's thought. "It's Chris. I forgot to call him."

She lifted the phone and hit the button. "Hi, I'm sorry. I lost track of time and forgot to call you. I plan to stay here and do a few things while you take your parents to the ferry. I hope that doesn't—"

"Josie, why? My parents look forward to saying goodbye, and all Ellie's talked about today is what the three of us can do."

"But I thought—"

"Stop thinking, and get over here. We leave shortly, and we all want you to be here."

Despite her need to protect herself from her concerns and emotions, she gave in. With little time available, she changed her clothes and hurried down Market Street. As she passed the boarded windows of shops and boutiques, that normally was packed with tourists and eager patrons purchasing clothing and gifts, often from Michigan, an empty sensation rolled down her back. This is how she would feel once she returned to lower Michigan where her life would slip back into the same mold she'd walked away from. Lots inside, but no one to know or care.

Self-pity. She shook her head as tension crawled up her back and settled into her neck. Why did these thoughts have to hit her today? She had to force herself to stay connected enough to enjoy the rest of her stay, but disconnected enough not to be hurt when she says goodbye.

Some of the snow had melted so her steps were less chancy for falling. She hurried past the houses near Cadette Avenue and made her turn onto French Lane. When she arrived, Chris stood on the porch and held open the door for his parents to roll out their bags and head to the ferry. She noticed they were each wearing the scarf she'd given them as a pre-Christmas gift. Ellie stood behind them, looking as if she'd lost her last friend. Josie knew the feeling.

He hurried down the steps and put his arm around her shoulder. "Thanks for coming. I hope I didn't—"

"I'm okay, Chris. Sorry that I disappointed you. I didn't—"

He leaned in closer to her ear. "No apologizing. You had your reasons." He gave her a squeeze, and though confusion clung to her mind, she didn't add anything to the situation. Instead she stood back and watched Gramps help Ellie with her coat. She came out of the house last and joined her grandparents on the sidewalk heading to Main Street.

She walked beside Chris who linked his arm with

hers, and let her mind think about Ellie and the plans they'd had to entertain her. Along the way, the sun shone against the white snow creating a diamond glitter as they passed, and a hint of disappointment filled her mind.

With snow, they could get out and ride the snowmobiles or put on snow shoes or even tackle cross country skis. Without it, she seemed to lose her spirit of adventure. Ellie would be disappointed and bored if she was like many other children who needed constant entertainment. But Ellie could be different. She showed creativity in many ways when she played, and that was good for a child. Perhaps there was hope.

They stood back as Chris's parents hugged everyone goodbye, and his mother whispered in her ear how much she'd enjoyed meeting her. She returned the compliment, and it had come from her heart. They were nice people.

Ellie got double hugs, but she stuck close to Chris as if she wanted to make sure they weren't going to take her back with them. Once the ferry sailed from the slip, Ellie's spirit brightened, and she skipped around them, continuing to wave her hand as if that assured her that her grandparents were on their way.

Chris appeared to notice too, since he gave a head-toss toward Ellie with a wink in her direction. She let her grin be her response. As they headed back, Ellie jostled between them, took their hands and lifted her feet, wanting them to give her a swing forward.

Chris stopped in mid-step. "Are you trying to break our arms, Ellie?"

She tilted her head toward him and tittered. "I can't break your arms."

"Maybe." He smiled back. "You're heavier than you think, and Josie's delicate."

Josie chuckled at his comment, but he was correct. Ellie probably weighed close to forty pounds, but when she had to lift the girl totally with her arms, she felt the weight. "Are you bored, Ellie?"

She released their hands and spun around to face them. "I don't know."

"That means you don't have anything to do, and you want to do something fun."

She gave a decisive nod. "Let's make snow angels."

Chris put his hand on her arm and drew her closer. "Look at the snow, Sweetie. What do you see?"

Ellie curled up her nose and shrugged. "Melty stuff."

"Correct. If you tried to make a snow angel, it would be like floating in a pool and swinging your arms and legs. It's too wet to make anything today, but it's supposed to snow tonight. Look up at the sky." He pointed toward the darkening clouds. "They're filled with fresh snow."

She clapped her hands. "Good." But when she stopped her applause, she focused on Josie. "But what can we do today?"

The look on her face broke Josie's heart. Her mind hit a wall, but when she looked up and spotted what was in front of them, she had the answer. "I know. Let's go to the library and find some books. Do you like fairytales?"

"Cinderella?"

"Sure, and maybe Rapunzel. Do you know her story?"

She shook her head. "Did the prince kiss her back to life?"

"Not Rapunzel. That was Sleeping Beauty." She shifted her gaze to Chris. "Is that okay?"

"Sure it's a great idea." He pointed to the building ahead of them. "I think they're open." He grasped Ellie's hand and she took the other as they crossed the street.

♥

Chris stirred the spaghetti sauce in the kitchen and listened to Josie read Rapunzel to Ellie. "What did the witch say, Ellie."

Ellie giggled. "Rapunzel, Rapunzel, let down your hair to me."

"That's right, and then what happened?"

Ellie continued to tell the story about the handsome prince as he continued to prepare their dinner, but his mind put faces on the characters. Rapunzel had the uncanny appearance of Josie, except with very long hair, her child was Ellie, and he became the prince who found her as he wandered blindly through the forest. Her tears washed his eyes, and he had sight again, and he, Josie and Ellie, lived happily ever after.

He cringed and rolled his eyes at himself for his ridiculous thoughts. He and Josie had met not that many weeks earlier, and yet he felt he'd known her forever. But when he tried to make strides with their relationship, either she backed away or he did. He closed his eyes, longing to make sense of the future. What was meant to be?

"Daddy Chris."

His head shot upward as Ellie bound into the kitchen. "Can I help with dinner? Josie and I need a break."

"You do?" He noticed her eyes focused behind him, and when he turned Josie stood inside the doorway seeming to size up the situation.

"Do you need a salad or anything? Ellie and I are willing to help."

"Sure. Greens and tomatoes are in the fridge. I'm sure you'll find some other salad items."

Ellie skipped to her side and the two chattered and laughed as they made the salad. He checked the pasta and it was ready, and the sauce smelled so good his stomach rumbled.

He turned toward the salad makers, and his chest tightened realizing how happy Ellie seemed as she worked with Josie. She did miss a woman in her life. Children could deal with so much, but in their heart, he guessed they preferred to have a mom and a dad. "How's the salad?"

"Good, Daddy Chris. See." She held up the bowl and he spotted olives and some red peppers along with the greens and tomato.

"Then it's time to eat." Josie finished the last item in the salad, and set it on the kitchen table while he drained the pasta and put the sauce in a large bowl. When everything was on the table, he sent Ellie to tell Gramps that dinner was ready, and when she left, he closed the distance between him and Josie.

"Thanks for spending so much time with Ellie. I'm beginning to realize that I can't fill the hole in her life alone. I always thought I could...or maybe I wanted to think that."

"You've done a great job, Chris. Don't question yourself about that. I admire what you've done, and you've raised a beautiful little girl who's loving and creative. She's an amazing young lady even at four years old. And smart."

"She is smart. My brother was intelligent, and Mindy too. I give them the genetic credit for that."

"But you encouraged it in Ellie, Chris. Those abilities can be stifled if not encouraged and aided. Give yourself credit."

He shrugged, wanting to end the conversation. Compliments weren't something he accepted easily, and he suspected she was giving him more credit than due. "She's a good girl."

Josie drew in a breath and shook her head as if she gave up on him, and if it had to be that way, at least the compliments would end.

Gramps wandered in with Ellie skipping beside him, and they settled around the table while the scent of garlic and herbs filled the air. Ellie folded her hands and said a childhood table prayer he'd learned long ago, and he thanked her. She rarely remembered the prayer but today. for some reason, it seemed important to her.

"This is good, Chris." Josie held a fork over her plate filled with a spiral of pasta noodles and sauce. "It's a real treat to eat a home cooked meal that I don't have to make. Rose prepares my breakfast each morning, but otherwise, here on the Island, I'm eating here or out. That's quite a treat."

"It's a treat for me, too."

A frown popped to her face, as if she didn't agree...or maybe didn't understand.

"How can it be a treat?" A frown creased her brow. "You did all the work."

"But I did it for people I love and care about. Plus,

I don't mind cooking for an appreciative group, and Gramps always enjoys my cooking." He turned to his granddad. "Don't you Gramps?"

"Now, you have me on the spot. I suppose I have to say yes." Then he chuckled and gave Josie a wink. "To be honest, it's a real pleasure to have Chris cook. When he's not here, I'm the chief cook and bottle washer, as they say. And I'm alone. Having all of you here is like a continual holiday."

"Speaking of holidays, Gramps. I need to talk to you about the tree."

His granddad's face puckered as it always did about putting up a Christmas tree.

But Ellie perked up hearing him. "Christmas tree?"

He nodded. "That's what I mean, Sweetie."

"Can I help? Can Josie and I help, Daddy Chris."

"I couldn't pick out a tree without you, Ellie."

She turned her head toward Josie. "Or without Josie. You need us both."

"I guess I do."

Gramps puckered expression vanished as he slapped his knee. "Good. That means you don't need me, and I'm all for that. Standing out in the cold and looking at trees isn't my idea of fun."

"Gramps." Ellie let out a squeal. "It is fun. You can come too."

"Now I put my foot in it didn't I?" He dug his fork into the pasta. "Ellie, I think I'll enjoy it even more when you surprise me with the tree you pick out."

Her face brightened. "A surprise. Okay. We'll surprise you, Gramps. That will be really fun."

Chris gazed at Josie and had to agree. Picking out a Christmas tree with her would be fun.

Chapter 7

When Josie cornered Chris alone in the kitchen, she lowered her voice. "What's the deal about the Christmas tree and Gramps?"

He lifted one shoulder. "Since Grandma died, he's ignored most Christmas decorations. I'm not here for the holidays usually, but when I am I try to motivate him. I think Ellie was the trick this time. He knew he couldn't disappoint her by not having a tree."

"Then I'm glad she is here." Memories filled her mind as her spirit sank. "You know when I'm not with family, I suppose I'm the same. I have one little ceramic tree that I put out and plug in. It has lights and that's my Christmas tree. Holidays aren't fun alone, and they do bring back—"

"Too many sad thoughts." Chris rested his hand on her arm. "After Gary and Mindy were gone, I didn't want to face Christmas, especially having to put on a happy face for Ellie. It's hard, but you know, I forced myself, and once the tree was up and our stockings hung on the fireplace, I could smile, and it became easier."

"Thanks for telling me. Gramps is also teasing and coming up with playful comments, and I don't picture him sad and—"

"He puts on a good front when other people are around. I'm the one who saw it, and it did break my heart. I loved Grandma. She was the sweetest, and she sure cracked the whip with Gramps. She got him up and doing things. Now, he sits too much, but—"

"Then it's our job to get him moving too. Do you think we can?"

"Ellie would have the best shot, I think."

"Okay, let's see what we can do."

He slipped his arm around her shoulders and drew her close. "You are a magician, Josie. You've brightened my world and Ellie's."

"Pooh. You're the one who's made me happy, Chris. I'd be home by now missing all the joy of Christmas on the Island, but you came to my rescue and—"

"See, Josie, that's where you're wrong. You came to my rescue." He leaned down and kissed her cheek. The warmth washed through her, and the longings she'd experienced—longings she didn't want to face— multiplied.

"Daddy Chris." Ellie skipped into the kitchen. "Christmas tree." She beckoned him to follow her, but when he didn't move, she stopped. "Aren't we going?"

"We are, but you'll have to wait a while. We have things to do first."

Her smile slipped to a pout. "I don't want to do things first."

"Sorry, Ellie." Chris leaned down to face her. "But

that's life. Sometimes we have to wait."

Ellie turned to her, the girl's eyes begging for help.

Josie stepped to her side and eased her closer. "Did you know that waiting can be days or hours or lots of times only a minute?"

"How many days?" Ellie's plaintive expression almost made Josie laugh.

"That depends, but Daddy Chris doesn't mean days."

"Years?" Her face puckered, and Josie drew her into her arms.

"No. I said sometimes it's only minutes. That means soon."

She tilted her head up to Chris. "Are we going soon?"

He grinned. "Ellie, my sweet, yes, soon. I want to make sure we can find the tree ornaments."

Ellie shifted toward Josie. "What's ornaments?"

"Christmas decorations to hang on the tree."

Chris couldn't hide his quiet chuckle. "And strings of lights. I'm guessing they're in the attic, but I can ask Gramps."

A smile grew on Ellie's face. "Cuz we have to put them on the tree so it's pretty."

"Right." He glanced at Josie. "Let me finish here, and then we can ask Gramps."

Ellie turned and skipped out of the kitchen without a word.

Josie studied Chris a moment. "I never realized how having a child means the adult has to explain everything."

"True. That's how they learn, but sometimes it's tedious. I've had to learn patience."

"Ah. I need a lesson in that, too."

"Good. Then I'll let you answer her questions. I want to give you the opportunity."

She gave him a playful swat and spun around to join Ellie who she guessed was bugging Gramps already.

♥

Chris pulled down the ladder in the bedroom closet and eased up the steps, hoping to find the pull string to turn on the attic light.

"Be careful." Josie stood below him holding the drop ladder as if it weren't built in.

He pushed the trap door out of the way and heaved himself on the temporary floor boards. The attic was lit by only one bare light bulb, but Gramps told him that's where the Christmas stuff was kept.

A strand hit the side of his face, and he grinned, happy to pull the string and get some light other than the small windows on each end of the attic. The window grime impeded the sunshine. He stepped deeper into the storage area and spotted two plastic boxes of red and green. If that wasn't a hint, nothing was. He grinned and eased his way across the thin board. When he lifted the lid, strings of tree lights were coiled together and boxes below of colorful balls. He lifted one to the opening in the floor and looked down. "Josie?"

She moved closer and gazed up at him. "Find anything?"

"I did, but I'll need help getting this down. There are two boxes, not heavy, but cumbersome. He shifted the box to the edge so she could see it. "What do you think?"

"I can handle it."

Ellie darted beneath the opening and gazed up with a grin. "I can help, too."

"You can help by letting Josie get closer to the ladder. I'll come down and then lift this as low as I can, and hopefully…"

"Not hopefully. And I will take it and put it on the floor."

"Okay." Though she looked confident, he hoped she could do it without dropping all the fragile balls." He scooted over and pulled the other box close to the edge and then took a few steps down the ladder, until he had to stretch to reach the first box. He pulled it halfway over the edge, lifted it down between him and the rungs and took another couple of steps down until he could hand the box to Josie.

"Got it." She grasped the edges and lowered it to the floor.

Relief swished through him. He shouldn't have doubted her. He returned closer to the top and followed the same procedure and soon, the two boxes were sitting beside the ladder on the floor. "Good job, Josie."

"You did the hardest part." She stood beside the boxes as he descended the ladder and flipped the ladder back up.

Ellie had already taken the lid off one of the boxes and began pulling out the lights.

"Don't tangle them, Ellie. Okay? Now that we know we have lights and some decorations, let's get ready for tree hunting." He scooted the boxes against the wall.

She bounced beside him. "Can I help chop the tree?"

He looked heavenward, picturing her heaving an ax

and cutting off her foot. "These trees are already chopped. We just have to look at them and pick out our favorite."

"Who chopped it?"

He motioned toward Josie. She could take a turn.

She caught his action, gave a quick head shake, and turned away. "I have no idea, Mr. Banks."

Ellie faltered and looked around. Chris chuckled. "Josie is teasing me, Ellie. I'm Mr. Banks."

She grinned and caught on with a titter. Since she hadn't pressed him for an answer to her question, he let it drop. He knew who sold the trees but had no idea who chopped them down or from where, but he guessed it was somewhere in Saint Ignace.

"Are you ready, Ellie?" She skipped around him before heading for the door.

"Hold on. You need a coat." He motioned to her bare arms.

She gave him a silly grin and hurried to the closet where she pulled out her jacket. He followed and took his coat from a hook inside the door and then located Josie's. "Here you go." He tossed it to her, and she pulled her scarf from the sleeve and her gloves out of the pocket and slipped them on.

"It's an easy walk." He motioned for them to head outside, and on the sidewalk Josie caught up with him.

"Where is it?"

He pointed down the block. "Right here. Market Street and Cadette. The Junior class sells them as a fund raiser, I suppose."

In only a few minutes, they reached the tree lot. Before Chris could get organized, Ellie had vanished. "Drat. Did you see where she went?"

"I didn't, but I'm sure she's in the lot."

They headed in different direction while his frustration grew. A couple minutes passed before he heard Josie's voice. "Ellie's here, Chris."

He turned as they came around the corner of a row of trees. "Ellie, don't walk away. You need to stay with us so we can pick out a tree together."

"I found one, Daddy Chris." She beckoned him to follow her.

Though not happy, he covered his upset and followed her down the row until she stopped and pointed. He gazed about twelve feet into the air, looking at the biggest tree on the lot, he was sure. "Ellie, this tree is for one of the churches or a place with a very high ceiling. I agree it's pretty, but it would take up the whole living room and have to be cut in half or we would cut a hole in the ceiling."

"You can't, Daddy Chris. But you said I could pick the tree and this is the one—"

He moved closer and turned her to face him. "I said we would all pick out the tree, and you can't have this one because it won't fit in the house."

"But it's pretty." She turned to Josie. "Do you think it's pretty?"

"It's very pretty, but your Daddy Chris is right, Ellie. The tree is way too big for Gramps house. But let's look for one even prettier than this one, that will fit."

She considered that a moment, her chin almost touching the ground, and then lifted her head. "Okay."

Chris gave Josie a subtle pat, thanking her for her help. When Ellie wanted something, he'd found it hard to say no to her, but this was easy. The size removed any possibility of yes. This time he took Ellie's hand but allowed her to point out the kind of tree she liked. Big was obviously one of her preferences. He couldn't help but chuckle.

Josie walked around a corner and beckoned to them. "Ellie, look at this tree."

She meandered toward her as if her interest had waned, but when she saw the tree, she perked up. "It's not too big."

"Right, it's just a couple feet taller than me, and that means it won't touch the ceiling, and we can put a star or an angel on the tree."

"Angel." Ellie's response burst from her lungs. "Maybe it will be one right from heaven."

Her heart stood still, and she slipped her arm around Ellie understanding the child's need. "Angels on the tree aren't real angels, but they remind us that we all have a guardian angel who watches over us. That angel is from heaven, Ellie."

The child nodded. "It's my mommy, isn't it?"

"I don't know but it might be, Sweetheart."

"It is."

Josie held her response. Ellie needed to feel that her mom and dad were watching over her, and letting her believe could do no harm, she hoped. "Do you like this tree?"

"It's pretty, but what about those trees?"

She pointed to another row of trees, with thicker branches and bulkier. Still the tree could fit the house. "Do you want to look at those?"

Ellie nodded and rushed past the trees around her, her eye obviously on something else, but when Chris appeared at the end of the row, Josie stayed back and let him handle the tree selection.

Her mind muddied in the angel situation, and she hoped she hadn't stirred up a problem or misled Ellie just to make her happy. Being a child's guardian or parent created one of the most important and difficult jobs she could imagine. She'd given it no thought in the past, but now, things had changed. The responsibility seemed overwhelming, and she was at a loss.

Wandering among the trees, she spotted some she liked. Her favorites were the ones that had some open spaces to hold larger ornaments rather than the neat ones with pruned limbs that seemed the perfect shape. After a few minutes, she took a turn, having no idea which way Ellie and Chris had gone. For all she knew, they may have bought the tree and left, forgetting about her.

"There you are."

She pulled her head up to see Chris waving from between two trees with Ellie at his side. "I figured you had plenty of help."

"Not so. Ellie wants to make sure you like the tree too."

Her gaze shifted to Ellie standing beside what many have named a "Charlie Brown" tree. It's limbs were ragged with different lengths and those open spaces that she loved. "Is this the one, Ellie?"

"If you like it too." Ellie grinned with an expression that indicated she loved it. Josie shifted and glanced at Chris.

He gave her a subtle shrug. "It's her favorite."

She pressed her lips together to waylay her laugh. "It's beautiful."

A frown flickered on his face. "Really?"

"It's our favorite kind of tree, isn't it, Ellie."

Ellie beamed. "It's our favorite, Daddy Chris."

"Okay. If both of you say so." He reached into his pocket. "I'll pay for it and have someone bring it to the house."

He surprised her. "We can't carry it? It's not that far."

"They have a dray that will bring it right to the house." He eyed the tree and then her. "I don't know if we could carry it or not."

"Ask the guy over there, that's taking the money. Or we can test it and see if I can handle one end."

Chris stood a moment as if weighing her idea even more than weighing the tree. "Let's see."

They waved at the young man, and he wandered over and eyed the one they'd selected. "You want this one?" Curiosity sounded in his voice. "Really?"

"We do. Really." She hoped her tone of voice let him know they were serious.

"We'll deliver it tomorrow for you, if that works."

Josie gave Chris's arm a poke. He glanced at her and then the student. "We thought we could carry it, perhaps. We live a couple house down on French Lane."

The teen looked that way and paused. "Maybe. I can wrap it in net and it will be easier to handle. Do you want to test it?"

Chris nodded, and the young man lifted the tree and carried it to the tree wrapper. The net bound it into a compact bundle. He eyed it and then her. "Let's see your muscles."

She rolled her eyes. "And we have Ellie. She can carry the middle."

"Oh, yes, that will make a big difference."

Ellie heard his proposal and bounced beside him, ready to carry it herself if she could.

Josie stood near the tree top and Chris lifted the lower part of the tree, then the young man let the weight of the tree go into her arms. "Not bad."

Ellie stood in the middle, her arms stretched up, her face glowing as if she were carrying it by herself.

"What do you think?" Chris studied her a moment. "You look okay. How about if we take a few steps."

"I'm ready." She grasped the top about a foot down and hung on. Chris gave a nod, and she stepped ahead while he followed, and Ellie kept her arms raised in the middle which looked as if she at least helped them keep their balance.

"We're good." Josie eyed him before heading down Market Street. As she moved the weight became heavier, but waiting for tomorrow to decorate wasn't part of their plans. Or it wasn't part of her plans.

When they reached French Lane and made the turn, victory was close at hand until she tripped over the edge of the sidewalk and tumbled into a slushy snow bank. Chris lowered the end of the tree to the ground and hurried to her side while Ellie had been nearly knocked over by her sudden drop to the ground.

Chris gave Ellie a pat as he passed her. "Are you okay?"

"Only my pride is hurt." She didn't want to mention that her bottom was wet and had felt the concrete through her clothing.

"Good. I'll help you up." He shifted the tree and helped her stand.

"Sorry. And we're almost there." She felt her

backside and realized she would have to go back to Cottage Inn to change clothes.

"'Almost' doesn't help." He grinned at her. "A few more yards and we did it."

She bent down and grasped her end of the tree while he lifted the bottom and Ellie raised her arms back to the middle. This time they walked more slowly while she took each step with less confidence, but when they reached Gramps, they'd conquered the job.

Chris lugged the tree by himself to the porch. "We should let this stand until tomorrow, really, so it has a chance for the limbs to fall into their natural place. I think I'll move it to the back porch since it's covered."

"Tomorrow?" She sounded as pitiful as the look on Ellie's face.

"But Daddy Chris, I thought—"

"I should have told you that it needs time to sit a bit before putting it inside. I'm sorry, but we'll find something fun to do today, and then tomorrow, we can get started early in the day."

She and Ellie gazed at him without comment.

"Let's get inside and I'll move this around to the back." Chris opened the front door and though she took the steps up, she remembered she couldn't sit down inside without a plastic garbage bag under her. "Chris, I think I should go home and—"

He waved her words away and beckoned her inside. When she stepped in, Ellie started to giggle. "Josie has wet pants."

Wanting to melt through the floor, she managed to smile. "That's because I fell into the mushy snow. Remember when I said we can't make snow angels because the snow was melting."

Ellie nodded. "But you fell in it, and wet your pants."

She wanted to correct Ellie on her wording, but the child was four...almost five so why bother.

When she faced Chris, his expression caused heat to roll up her neck. "Seriously. I landed in that mush, and—"

He held up his hand like a traffic cop. "Just teasing, Josie."

"Just teasing? Just embarrassing me is what you should say. I said I needed to go home and—"

"Don't worry. Wait here." Chris hurried away as he called to Gramps.

She cringed. He had to tell Gramps about her fall too. She shook her head, waiting for Gramps to come in and add to her discomfort, but instead, Chris returned with clothes on his arm. "Gramps' cousin Rosie left more than that jacket. She has these pants or these." He held up two pair of casual pants like ones she used to go for a run.

"What don't you have of Rosie's?"

He grinned. "I didn't find an evening gown, but then on the island we don't really need those in winter."

"I'm glad." She eyed the two pair of slacks and took the blue ones. They went better with her blouse. "Tell Rosie thanks, and you could ask her to bring an evening dress at least. You never know."

Chris grinned and grasped the other pair she returned. "Use my bedroom to change if you want...or wherever you prefer."

She nodded and headed down the hall to the bathroom. She slipped out of her wet clothes and stepped into Rosie's dry ones. Eyeing herself in the mirror, she ran her fingers through her hair, and wished she'd brought her purse in with her. Curious what Chris had planned, she hung her wet slacks across the shower bar and headed down the hallway to the living room.

"Anyone hungry?" Gramps stood inside the kitchen door wearing a grin.

She stopped and took a deep breath. "What's cookin', Gramps." When the name slipped out, she realized that the name Harry had long since vanished from her vocabulary. Since she'd been spending more time at his house than at the Cottage Inn, Gramps just seemed to be the appropriate name to call him.

"Soup. That's what's cookin'." He motioned her toward the kettle on the stove.

She wandered in and tried to guess before she saw it. "Is that potato soup?"

"Half is." He grinned.

"Half?" She leaned closer and spotted the golden colored dots. "And corn. It's potato corn chowder." Excitement rose in her voice since he'd made one of her favorite meals. "If I'm right, Gramps, you're getting a huge hug."

He opened his arms and she stepped in, wrapping her arms around him and even kissing his cheek. "My favorite. Truly my favorite."

"If this is treatment for making your favorite, Josie, I'm going to be cooking meals for you as often as I can."

She chuckled at his joyful response. "You make me laugh, Gramps."

"And you make me happy, Girl. You're one of the nicest people I know."

"Me?" She studied his face thinking he was teasing

again, but he wasn't. "Why do you say that?"

"Well, my girl, first look at Ellie. She's enjoying your company so much. She's smiling most of the time and talking about you as if you're her favorite storybook princess."

"That's a sweet compliment." She wondered if she was Cinderella, Snow White or Sleeping Beauty.

"But it's more than that. You play with her, talk to her like she's important. You've become like a mother which is something she doesn't have."

A knife dug into her heart. Though his words were meant as a compliment, her involvement with Ellie could end up hurting the child. No matter what, she was not Ellie's mother and never would be. She would be another woman who vanished from her life when it was time to go.

"Did I say something that hurt you, Josie?"

She jerked at his question. "No Gramps, it's just that I'm not Ellie's mother, and she's been happy with Chris, but now I've reminded her that she's lost her mother. She's always talking about angels. When I leave, I'll be another woman who vanishes again, and that's horrible. I wish I hadn't gotten so involved with her now. How can I explain when I leave? She's a smart little girl and acts older than she is, but she's still a child,"

"So why must you walk away? No one said you can't stay in touch."

She eyed the older man, surprised he doesn't understand. "It's not practical. Chris has a life. I have a life. Ellie fits in his life, and he lives in one place and I live in another."

"You're not that far apart, Josie. Chris lives in your

area. Sure, it's another city but it's not a thousand miles or even a hundred miles away. The only thing that can keep you apart is your decision."

The knife deepened. She drew in a ragged breath and swallowed her excuses. "I don't know, Gramps. I love it here. I wish I could live here, but time will tell once we're back. Life has a way of tangling us in ruts. I've been in one for years, and this trip took one foot out of it."

Gramps grinned. "How about letting Chris take the other foot out of the rut. Life might be fun. Adventurous even."

"Hey, Gramps." Chris's voice shot into the kitchen before he did. "There you are." He looked at Josie. "I thought you got lost."

"Nope, but she smelled my soup." Gramps lifted the lid and swished the scent toward Chris. "Let's eat. I'm hungry."

Chris meandered to the pot and looked at it. "Gramps, I think that's your award-winning soup. I'm ready." He tilted his head toward the door. "I'll get Ellie."

"I'll get her, Chris." Josie passed him and went to the living room. Ellie was seated on the floor looking at a book. "What's the book about, Ellie?"

She held up the cover as Josie read the name. "'Poetry for Children.' That sounds interesting. I have a book of poems that I've had so long it's falling apart. I loved those poems when I was your age, and I still love them."

"Can you read some to me?"

"I will, but I think Gramps has dinner ready. Let's eat and then we can do the poems."

She gazed at the pages a moment longer and then followed Josie into the kitchen where Gramps was filling the soup bowls.

"Can I help?" Josie moved to Chris's side where he was cutting big hunks of French bread, spreading on butter with flecks of garlic and tossing the pieces on a grill. In moments, the garlic butter had melted and turned golden brown.

"Nope, I'm done, but you can help me after dinner. I have an idea."

"Idea?"

He only smiled and left her with her imagination.

Chapter 8

Chris's comment to Josie clung in his mind. His idea wasn't that great, and any other ideas escaped him. "Gramps, your soup tastes great." He grasped the large ladle and refilled his bowl.

When he finished, Ellie shoved hers toward him. "Could I have a little more?"

"You sure can." He dipped another ladle into her bowl, and then he grinned when he noticed Josie had her bowl in hand ready to ladle her own, Instead, he did it for her.

Gramps watched them with a broad smile. "I guess the soup was a hit."

"It's delicious, Gramps." Josie lowered the bowl to table and picked up her spoon. "And it's perfect for a colder day."

"Speaking of cold days, let's go through the ornaments I found in the attic and make sure the lights work and the ornaments aren't broken. They've been there for years. If we need more, we can take a walk later or tomorrow and see what we can pick up."

"I like doing an inventory, but other than the strings of lights, I have another idea, but it will mean going out into the cold."

Ellie's interest showed in her wide eyes.

Chris turned his attention to Josie. "What's the plan?"

"Let's make some ornaments."

"Can we?" Ellie bounced in her chair her hands just missing the soup bowl as her spoon flipped out onto the floor. She lowered her eyes, her smile fading. "Sorry." She slipped from the chair and retrieved the spoon.

Josie rose and reached for it. "I'll get you a clean one, Ellie."

She handed it to Josie who opened the silverware drawer and brought out another one. "I see you like the idea, Ellie." She handed her the clean spoon and returned to her place at the table.

Ellie bounced her head with a big smile. "We can make angels and stars and—"

"And decorate pinecones, if we can find some in the woods."

Gramps chortled. "You can find tons of them, I'm sure. I don't think the snow is that heavy that you can't see them."

"But that's a cold walk." Chris's neck turned from Josie to Ellie and back. "It'll take a while to get to the pine trees."

"I don't think they're that far off, Chris. Cadette Avenue and around the golf course have lots of pines. We should find them there, and we don't need that many."

He shrugged. "Maybe you're right."

She arched her eyebrow. "What do you mean

'maybe?'"

Gramps guffawed and slapped the table top so hard he made the bowls rattle.

"This place is dangerous." Chris shook his head, unable to contain his grin.

With their plan stated, Ellie grasped her bowl and put it on the countertop. "I'll get warm clothes on, okay?"

"Don't rush, Ellie. We need to go through the ornaments first."

She lowered her head as her disappointment made itself known. One thing he'd learned about kids, they want action, not waiting. "It won't take long."

"Okay." Her frown faded.

Josie gathered the dishes while Chris carried the rest of the soup into the kitchen. In moments, the soup was ready to refrigerate after and the dishes were in the washer. Gramps had already settled into his recliner across from the TV, and Josie, with Ellie beside her, headed for the bedroom where they'd left the boxes.

When he entered, Ellie had already pulled off one of the box lids while Josie attempted to monitor her exuberance. He didn't interfere but watched them work together. When the lights were piled on the floor, Josie found the end of the string and he plugged it in. "Nothing."

"Ellie can you sit right there." Josie pointed to a spot next to the coiled lights. "And look at every place a blub should be to make sure there are none missing."

He loved seeing the way Josie managed to come up with things for Ellie to do that were easy enough and yet made her feel important.

Ellie gave one of her big nods and went to work,

while Josie and he went through the other lights and tightened the bulbs. Eventually they had four strings working and two that seemed hopeless.

"What do you think, Chris." Josie pointed to the two useless strands.

"Can we buy new ones?" Ellie held a broken strand and eyed the bulbs.

Chris gazed at the four working strands and shrugged. "I'm not sure how many we need." He motioned to the boxes of other Christmas decorations. "Are there enough ornaments to make you both happy?"

"Daddy Chris, we're going to make some, remember?"

He'd hoped that had been forgotten, but Josie had the same smile on her face as Ellie so he knew he'd lost the battle. "I suppose we'd better get ready to look for pinecones, and then we need to stop at the store too."

Josie nodded. "We need paint and glitter, plus some card stock and colored markers."

"I like glitter." Ellie's gleeful expression made him smile despite his lack of enthusiasm. When he spotted Josie's same joyful appearance, the truth hit him. Two beautiful females and one man meant he would lose every battle. Except being with these two wasn't a loss. He'd been given a gift even though he didn't like to admit it.

♥

Once outside, Josie admitted the cold weather permeated her bones. A chill ran up her back, and though she tried to hide it, she failed.

"See, I told you." Chris winked and drew to her side. "Will this help?" He slipped his arm around her waist and drew her closer. "Do you have a sweater under that jacket?"

She ignored him for a moment, although by doing that, he knew she hadn't. "I wasn't thinking."

Ellie bounced in front of them, carrying a paper bag they'd found in the kitchen and searching beneath every tree no matter if it was coniferous or deciduous.

Chris shook his head and grinned. "She's eager."

"I know. It's fun to watch her be excited."

His eyes met hers, and an unexpected excitement raced up her spine. "Ellie has a wonderful spirit. I hope it rubs off."

"On me?" Chris tilted his head with a look she didn't understand.

"No. On me. I've spent much of my life accepting what happens rather than deal with it. I sort of go with the flow. Always afraid to step out of the safety zone."

"Which means that you're staying here when your friend couldn't come represents one of those times you took a step."

"A big one, Chris." She gazed at the sidewalk a moment. "A very big step."

"Why? What gave you the courage?"

Her heart gave a tug. "Do you really want to know?"

"I do, although I can guess that you'd made reservations so you—"

"No. I could have cancelled the reservations, but I didn't." She eyed him a moment. "And you want to know why, right?"

"I would love to know."

She studied him a moment, gaining the nerve to tell him. "Because of you."

His eyes widened as if someone jumped out of a hiding place. "Me? You didn't know—"

"You picked up my coat from the floor, and you joined me at the table. We talked, and I liked you. In all honesty, you made me feel comfortable and confident for some reason."

"I did? Thanks for letting me know. I never think of myself as much of anything that's special. I just do my job and take care of Ellie. Nothing exciting."

"But that is exciting, Chris. You're raising a lovely little girl, working to support both of you, and still being kind to a stranger like me. You smiled, and you offered to be my tour guide for no reason, and you've been more than that. We've become friends." She paused and studied his expression. "At least I think we're friends."

"Good friends, Josie. I like you, too. More than I can say."

His comment caught her off guard, and she wasn't sure she understood what that meant. "I like you a lot."

Chris's serious expression morphed to a grin. "I'm glad."

Her chest tightened while her pulse danced. She gazed at him admiring his good-looks which she'd tried not to notice. Not only was he special—kind and fun and generous—but he was actually handsome. His eyes had a depth that drew her in the same way as stars add beauty to the evening. She'd tried to control her feelings, but he'd captured her in a way she couldn't explain.

He didn't speak, and he didn't have to. His eyes said all she needed to know.

"Come on." Chris beckoned to Ellie who bounced

in front of them, waving her arms toward the line of trees along the road.

Chris drew in a breath as if awakening from a dream and grinned. "I guess this conversation will continue later."

He hugged her waist, arched his eyebrow and let his hand slip off her. "We're coming, Ellie." An icy chill washed through Josie as they stepped apart, and his comment hung in the air like icicles, the meaning as cold as frozen snow.

Ellie skipped ahead, and when she turned toward them, her face glowed. "Look." She pointed below a tree at the edge of the Grand Hotel golf course.

Moving closer, Josie spotted the numerous pinecones waiting to be collected. She shoved a few in her pockets until she could get to Ellie's paper bag. "Let's see how many you have now."

Ellie added a few more to the sack and then skipped over and let her look inside.

"I think that's enough. We can let those dry in the house while we make a few other ornaments, and then we can decorate the pinecones."

Ellie's head popped up. "What other ornaments?"

Chris slipped behind Ellie and gave her a hug. "You'll find out."

"But…" Her playful pout appeared, but they only laughed.

"Patience, Ellie, my girl." Chris tousled her knit cap. "Let's head toward town and pick up the other supplies you'll need. I'm sure we'll find it all somewhere—the hardware store, Outfitters, Douds."

Time entered Josie's thoughts. "We can, or if you want me to shop, you can get Ellie back home and start drying the pinecones."

He shrugged. "If you make a list of what you need, I can do it. I know the stores better than you do, I'm sure."

She grinned and got the point. "Okay. Then it's back to Gramps' house for Ellie and me."

The thought of warmth inspired her to hurry along, and though they'd walked farther than the Grand Hotel, she flew back to French Lane. Once inside Gramps', she rubbed her arms back to life and kicked herself for not dressing warmer.

"List?" Chris extended his hand and gave her a wink.

Though she still preferred to go along since she knew what they needed, they both recognized that Ellie would want to go too and that meant more time wasted. "I'll make the list and let's hope I don't forget anything." She grasped a note pad and pen Gramps had on the kitchen counter and jotted down paint, glitter, glue, Christmas ribbon, card stock, colored markers, and Christmas stickers. "I hope this is it, Chris."

He looked at the list and rolled his eyes. "So do I."

♥

Chris made rounds through the stores that were open, grateful he'd found most everything Josie had listed. The woman amazed him. Why she wanted to get involved in creating ornaments sat in his mind like a rock. The easy way was to buy a few items. He'd already picked up four new strings of tree lights. He could have purchased whatever else they needed.

Yet he pictured a bag of store bought items, and then pictured Ellie and Josie sitting at the table side by side working together to create special ornaments to decorate the tree. Ellie had tons of energy, and her mind snapped with creative ideas like lightning. Pictures she'd drawn hung from the refrigerator and a cork board he'd put on the hallway wall. Ellie's talents had begun to blossom, and now he'd found someone who encouraged her to use her talents. Store bought could never compete with Ellie's handmade decorations.

Josie stepped into his world in a strange way, as if she'd been put there so he could pick up her jacket and draw her into his life. Not only her generosity and kindness filled his heart, but her beauty inside and out filled his thoughts. Her eyes, her hair, her slim frame, everything stuck in his mind as if attached with permanent glue. No matter what he did to replace the thoughts, they dropped to the ground while her loveliness etched to his brain.

They did need to talk, and when he made reference to that, he'd seen her flinch. That troubled him more than he admitted. He'd tried to pass it off, but the image remained.

His lungs emptied his pent-up breath, and he forced his eyes to the list. He gazed at his purchases and acknowledge that he had everything she needed.

He hoped.

By the time, he returned, Ellie and Josie were deep in their project. The table was covered with newspaper and the pinecones were strewn in various groups which made him curious. "What are you doing?"

Josie turned toward him. "What does it look like?" She grinned.

"We're waiting for you, Daddy." She pointed to the bags he carried.

But Chris stood still, stunned.

Josie looked at him, then shifted to Ellie who seemed to be unaware of what she'd called him, and back at Chris. "I guess Ellie told you what we're doing." She gave him a wink. "We're waiting for the glue and paint."

Still startled, he set the bags on the table and hoped to calm himself. "I think I got everything on the list."

Josie opened the sacks and lifted out the items he'd purchased, giving a nod to let him know he'd done a good job. "Wonderful. As far as I know, we have everything." She turned to Ellie. "Now we can get busy."

"Now we can get busy." Ellie gave him a decisive nod that made him and Josie chuckle.

"I'll get out of your way then, and you can surprise me. Tomorrow, we'll put up the tree and your surprises can be on display."

Ellie nodded. "We can hang the pinecones on the tree."

Chris gave Josie a wink and headed for the living room where he could think.

When he plopped onto the sofa, Gramps looked up. "What's wrong?"

He glanced at the doorway, wanting to keep his voice low, and shook his head. "Nothing's wrong." He rose and crossed over to Gramps chair and drew up the old rocking chair from the corner of the room. Once he sat, he lowered his voice and explained.

Gramps expression didn't change. "Daddy? Is that a surprise?"

"You know it is, Gramps. I've been Daddy Chris since she could talk. Gary referred to me as Uncle Chris, and when she got a year older, she changed it to

Daddy Chris. I've never been Daddy and never expected to be. That's why I'm confused. I don't know why it happened now."

"Think, Chris. She had a daddy and a mommy, and then she had none. Uncle Chris took over the daddy role, and she probably started to call for her daddy and then corrected it to Chris and you became Daddy Chris, but things are different now, if you really think about it."

He starred at Gramps with a blank face, he was certain. He had no idea what the difference was. "Explain, Gramps."

"You know what, Chris. I think I'll let you figure it out. You will. I know you will."

"You think so. I think you're far more certain than I am."

Gramps patted his arm. "Trust me."

He'd heard that before, and as much as he wanted to say he didn't trust him, Gramps' had a grip on many things far better than he did. He drew in air and closed his eyes. When he opened them, his grandfather only looked at him. "I have no choice, do I?"

Gramps shook his head. "You know I'm right."

He shrugged, but in his heart Gramps uncanny ability to comprehend life always surprised him. Yes, trust is what he would do.

♥

Josie finished the final strokes of gold paint on the last pinecone and let Ellie sprinkle on some of the silver glitter to look like glistening snow. They pinecones would be clustered in two or three with ribbon once they were all dry, and now she pulled out the cardstock to add a few other decorations that would give Ellie a chance to be totally creative.

"And I can do anything I want?" Ellie's eyes widened.

"You can." She held up a piece of blue cardstock. "I'm going to make stars. I'll cut them out and add some of the glitter to make them sparkle."

"Okay." Ellie leaned over and pulled out a piece of white paper. "I'm going to make an angel."

Josie's chest tightened. Once again, the child's parents had risen in the child's sweet mind. "I think an angel might be hard to make."

"I can do it." She gazed down at the cardstock in front of her. "But I might need help to make the wings."

"Okay, I can help you with that."

Ellie smiled and went to work while Josie drew a star shape on hers. She tried not to watch, fearful that she would correct Ellie or try to help her, and Ellie needed to do it herself unless she asked for help. That's how kids learn. At least, she knew that.

Her star, though a bit lopsided, looked okay and after she sprinkled on the blue glitter, it was pretty if she did say so herself. "What do you think, Ellie?" She held up the star.

"It's pretty." She grasped her project and lifted it. "Mine's pretty too."

Getting the first real look at the angel, Josie's heart skipped. "It's very pretty, Ellie, and it only needs one thing."

"Wings." Ellie nodded. "But you'll help me."

"I will." She picked up a piece of the white cardstock and studied it. "We could cut out a wing or I could pleat the paper so that the wing has folds in it. What would you like?"

A deep frown winkled Ellie's forehead, and she sat for a few moments as if making a decision that would change the world. "Can we do both?"

"Hmm?" She stared at the paper trying to imagine shaping a wing and folding, but then the way struck her. "I'll try." She sketched a wing shape with a wider middle and after she cut it out, she made small folds and smiled as the wing took form. "What do you think, Ellie?"

Ellie gave a big nod. "It's very pretty now, and it will make Mommy very happy."

"Anything you make would make your Mom and Dad very happy, Ellie. And you know why?"

Ellie studied her a moment and then shrugged.

"Because you made it. It's even more special."

Her face brightened. "I do."

"For sure. You can count on it."

Ellie clapped her hands and then helped Josie put the wings on the angel and used some glitter to make them sparkle.

Josie's heart filled with love for the young girl who wanted so badly to please her parents in heaven. The thought brought tears to her eyes, touched by the child and her joyful way of grieving and loving.

"Ellie." Chris stood in the kitchen doorway. It's getting late and it's bedtime for you, young lady. The only break you two had today was dinner, and that wasn't much."

Ellie gazed up at him, her face like a lost puppy. "Do I have to go to bed?"

"Don't you want to decorate the tree tomorrow?" He tilted his head. "I don't think you do."

"But Daddy Chris, I want to decorate the tree."

Ellie's pout appeared, and Josie struggled to not smile.

"Then, it's time to go to bed with no argument. Tomorrow will be a fun day."

Her pout sank to a frown, but she put down the colored marker, and, in slow motion, slipped off the chair. "Okay." Her head hanging, she ambled to the hallway leading to her bedroom.

Josie covered her mouth to avoid laughing out loud.

Chris gave her a wink. "I'll be back in a few minutes." He tilted his head toward Ellie and followed her down the hall.

Josie sat a moment, looking at all the decorations they'd made. Tomorrow they could finish the job in a short time and have fun decorating the tree. She located one of the paper bags and gathered up the glitter, paint and markers and moved them off the table.

Chris appeared and headed for the refrigerator. "Gramps went to bed so we have some private time. I started a fire in the fireplace earlier. Why not go in, and I'll be there in a minute."

She loved his planning. Private time. That was rare. But as she left the kitchen, she recalled his reference earlier to having time to continue their conversation. Instead of her eagerness to relax, she tensed not knowing if this conversation would be good or bad.

The living room eased her concern. The fireplace flickered in the dim lighting of a small lamp across the room, and someone had turned on background music of classic Christmas carols. The lilting melodies added to the warmth.

When Chris finally appeared, he carried two mugs, and the scent of chocolate filled the air. "Hot chocolate."

He handed her a cup, and she grasped the handle and drew in the rich scent. "Just what I needed."

"I thought so." He grinned and settled beside her on the sofa before taking a sip of the drink. "Thanks for doing so much for Ellie. She's having a wonderful time. I heard nothing in the bedroom except how you are just like a mommy. She's needed a woman's touch since her mom died. I do my best, but—"

"You are the best, Chris. Obviously, you can't be a mother, but you are a wonderful father figure with her. You are patient and generous with your time and your love."

"I try, but—"

"No but, Chris. You're an amazing man, and to her, you're a star. Accept the compliment. I understand, because I don't accept them well either, but please know that I'm being honest with you." She blew on the rising steam from her cup and sipped the edge.

"Then I'll be honest too. Ellie wanted me to listen to her prayers tonight, and along with her mom and dad and me, she prayed for you. She called you her second mommy."

Breath escaped her, and she closed her eyes, aware that her earlier fear had begun to happen. "Oh, Chris. What am I going to do? That poor child can't think of me as a mom. I'll be leaving and then—"

"We'll be leaving too, Josie." He set his mug on the lamp table. "You don't live that far from my home in the suburbs. Maybe you could stop by once in a while—if you wouldn't mind—or I could—"

"Mind? I wouldn't mind, Chris, but that will just make it worse. What if I decide to move or—"

"Or fall in love and—"

"No, that's not going to happen."

"Why is that so impossible?"

She studied his strained features, looking as if she'd attacked him. "I told you before that marriage is out of the question for me."

"But why? If you can't have children then—"

"That's not it." She looked into the mug and set it on the coffee table. "I don't know if I can have children or not, but I suppose I could. It's just that..." Her thoughts tumbled through her mind, and as she sorted her reason, it sounded weak and made little sense. "I have two sisters who married and are now divorced. That's not going to be me, so I decided—"

"Please don't tell me you've based a major life decision on your sisters' problems. Josie, you aren't your sisters."

"I know that. We're nothing alike really, but I think it's a genetic flaw."

He lowered his face to his hands and didn't respond. When he inched upward, his look tore at her senses. Her decision had been made years earlier. She'd lived with it. She gazed at him, wishing she'd had another reason. She shouldn't have said anything.

"It doesn't make sense to you, Chris, but divorce isn't an option for me. I don't believe in it. I think it hurts families, even extended families. And it especially hurts children. They spend their lives torn who to spend Christmas with, who to talk with when they have problems, who to trust, who to—"

"I agree with you, Josie. I don't take marriage lightly either, and that's what I wanted to talk with you about."

Her head shot upward. "What?"

"I'm taking a chance here, Josie, but I can't hide my feelings anymore. We both said that we liked each other a lot. Remember?"

"Yes, you've been wonderful, and I—"

"You've been wonderful too. I just told you how much I appreciate your showing interest and love to Ellie. But I have feelings too. We've known each other a short time, but we've spent quality time together, and I don't want to lose you."

"Lose me?" She studied his face and the depth of his emotions surprised her. "Chris, I meant everything I said about you, but this is a vacation and a unique location—the island is romantic and interesting—and do we know if it's the setting that has influenced the emotions?

Chris touched her hand and wove his fingers around hers. "Not for me."

Not for her either. She'd stood guard over her heart for years, and whatever happened between them sneaked up on her despite her staunch determination not to get involved. "I always stand guard over myself and my actions, but something happened here. My days were pure pleasure. I've looked forward to talking to Gramps and seeing Ellie, and spending time with you."

"Then let's be honest about what we have. It's special. You can't call it anything else, Josie."

He unwound his fingers and slid his arm around her back.

She weighed his comment, wanting to disagree. "You're right. I can't, Chris. What's happened here is different. And the best part is that I'm not afraid."

He drew her closer. "That means the world to me, Josie. Let's continue to enjoy the time we have and give us a chance. Can you do that?"

She lowered her head, her mind spinning with an I-don't-know response, but her heart telling her yes. When she lifted her chin, she gave a faint nod. "I'd like that, and if we changed now, Ellie would be very confused."

"Then you're doing this for Ellie." His voice grew dark.

"No, I'm doing it for me."

He used his finger to turn her face to his. "Do you mean that?"

She lost herself in his eyes. "You know I do."

Her longing grew, a dream that invaded her attempt to sleep arose, but this time it was real. She eased forward, lowering her lips to his, while his heartbeat throbbed against her chest. His fingers shifted against her back and a gentle sweep of his hand swayed with the rhythm of their hearts.

She drew back, startled at her daring to act on her unwanted dream, but today the dream had become reality. Better than any dream could have been. She'd never been kissed this way before.

The music had stopped, and when she straightened, Chris touched her cheek and his look melted her heart. "No music and cold chocolate, but it's perfect."

She grinned. "Better than perfect." She shifted and rose. "You handle the music, and I'll warm the chocolate in the microwave. We can start over."

"Over? No, that was a preview. Let's start where we left off."

She grasped his mug and hers, gave him a playful look and headed for the kitchen in total agreement. Tonight, she had thrown caution out the window, and the window would stay closed.

Chapter 9

Chris tossed off the blankets and swung his feet to the floor. He'd hoped to get some sleep, but sleep had evaded him. All night he'd drifted for a few moments and then woke reliving the kiss. He hadn't meant to come on that strong, but when she responded in the same way, his concern faded, and his confidence rose.

In the light of day, the truth would rise, and he prayed Josie would let him know that the kisses meant as much to her as they did to him. Her reasoning about not marrying didn't make sense to him, yet he'd never planned to marry either, not wanting to put anyone between him and Ellie. The child needed his attention and security. He'd promised himself to provide it in every way he could.

He blew out a stream of air and rose. Over-thinking his feelings was a waste of time. He didn't have to prove anything to himself. Josie was the one that needed proof of his feelings, and he hoped that time would answer her questions.

Ellie's voice sounded in the hallway, and he

suspected she'd already bugged Gramps to put up the Christmas tree. He grabbed his clothes and darted to the bathroom for a shower. The warm water washed away his tiredness, and once dressed, he was ready to face the day.

When he reached the kitchen, Ellie was at the table with scrambled eggs along with Gramps. "Good morning."

Gramps looked up. "If you're hungry, I made enough eggs for you too." He tilted his head. "They're in the pan."

He glanced at the eggs, noticing they were still warm. Once they were on the plate, along with a piece of toast, he settled beside them at the table.

"It's Christmas tree day, Daddy Chris."

"I know. I'll get busy after I eat." He jumped up having forgotten his coffee.

"But Josie and I still have things to finish."

"I thought everything was ready for the tree."

A slight frown touched her face. "Almost."

He shrugged. "It'll take a while to put up the tree and string the lights. You'll be done by then."

"Okay." She took another fork of eggs but played with them more than eating. "Where's Josie?"

He shook his head. "I suppose at the Cottage Inn having breakfast."

"Can we go there and get her?"

"No."

"Why?"

"Because she'll be here as soon as she can, and I'm going to put up the tree."

Ellie frowned again and stared at her plate.

"Do you remember the word patience, Ellie?"

Her eyes shifted from one direction to another as if she would find the word hanging somewhere in the room. "It means learning to wait without getting upset."

"I don't remember."

A grin flickered on his cheek, and he couldn't stop his chuckle. "I think you will if you really think about it."

"Can I have the paper, so I can do my decoration?"

He looked around the countertop and saw a bag tucked away in the corner. "Maybe that's it." He rose and opened the sack top. "Here it is. Markers, paper, glitter. This is what you want."

"Markers and a paper."

He dug into the bag and pulled out the items. "Here you go." He laid it on the table in front of her and returned to his breakfast. While he ate, Ellie kept busy with the markers, and he finished his food. Gramps had already excused himself, so he rinsed his plate and set it in the sink before searching for him.

Gramps sat in his living room recliner watching the morning news on TV. Chris stopped in the doorway, trying to think. "Gramps, do you know where the tree stand is?"

"In those boxes you found upstairs, I think. Didn't you find it?"

"I don't recall, but I'll check." He turned down the hallway and went into the bedroom where they'd left the boxes. He checked them with no luck. But before he took a step, another idea struck him. He pulled down the ladder and climbed up again, pushing away the attic door and easing his way through the ceiling opening.

"Where are you?"

Ellie's voice rose from the opening, and he looked

down at her. "I'm up here, looking for the tree stand."

"What's a tree stand?"

"It's something that holds the tree in place." Josie's voice greeted him. "Good morning." She stood below and waved. "I think I put the stand out on the porch with the tree."

"You did?" He lowered himself to the ladder, closed the trap door, and hurried down. He gave her a quick hug and headed for the porch where he found the stand.

Inside, Josie and Ellie were back at the table. Ellie concentrated on her drawing, while Josie seemed to be tying two or three pinecones together with ribbon. "I thought you were done with those."

She looked up. "Not quite. I like to put them in bunches." She held up the pinecones, glittering with gold flakes and tied with a red ribbon and then went back to work.

His pulse skipped, seeing her sweet smile and eagerness to finish the projects with Ellie so they could decorate the tree. "It's very nice, Josie. I'm glad you knew what to do with them."

"I think I learned about pinecones when I was close to Ellie's age. Maybe a little older but my mom taught me." Her smile faded as she glanced at Ellie. "This is the last one."

Ellie's focus had left her picture and turned to Josie. "And now you're teaching me to make them."

Her innocent smile, knotted his heart, but the knot tightened when he read Josie's expression. A frown hid below her taut grin.

"You have learned, Ellie, and you've done a good job." Josie's eyes remained on the red ribbon.

Chris flinched. Her tone sounded unnatural, and he prayed Ellie didn't notice. Instead of gawking at the stressful situation, he hurried to the enclosed porch and maneuvered the tree through the kitchen and into the living room. Though he'd started alone, Ellie joined him, leaving her artwork behind.

"Can we decorate now?" She bounced beside him as he found a place to prop the tree. "Can you go to the porch and bring me the tree stand."

"I'll try." She skipped back through the kitchen doorway.

He shook his head at his stupidity. Ellie had asked about a tree stand earlier, and now he'd sent her to get it. He stared at the doorway wondering what she would bring into the living room.

When she appeared, she carried the stand, and he burst into laughter. "Good job, Ellie. Now you know what a tree stand looks like."

She gave a big nod. "I do." She carried it across the room and set it on the floor.

Gramps wandered in with perfect timing. "Gramps, can you balance this tree while I tighten the bolts?"

"Sure thing." He hurried to Chris's side, eyed the tree, and held it in place while he got down on the floor and worked on the stand. "Let go, Gramps and tell me if it's straight."

Gramps stepped back a couple of yards. "Looks good to me.

Ellie skittered next to Gramps, and Chris grinned. "What do you think, Ellie?"

"It's good, Daddy."

His chest tightened hearing her again. Though he'd thought he should correct her the last time, making an issue of it would serve no purpose. Names were names. Love was love, and to him Ellie was his little girl.

He wiggled out from under the tree, stood and backed up to get a better view. "Okay, Gramps. We're a good team."

"Straight as a poker, I'd say."

Chris gave his granddad a high five and then put his hand on Ellie's shoulder. "Guess what."

"Is it time?"

He nodded. "Tell Josie."

"Josie." Ellie's voice pierced the air as she bounded across the room. "It's time to decorate."

Chris watched her vanish into the kitchen, assured that even the neighbors knew it was time to decorate.

♥

Josie gathered the ornaments they'd made and put them in a pile. "Coming, Ellie." They could put them on last. Ellie shot through the doorway, and as she rose she noticed the child's drawing and fought to keep from letting her face show her sadness. "We'll put our new decorations on last so we can get the best spots."

"The best ones." Ellie's smile broadened like the Cheshire Cat.

Her gaze swept over the drawing as she blocked the image and grasped Ellie's hand. They hurried into the living room, and then stopped. "Guess what, Ellie."

The child looked at the tree seeing Gramps and Chris passing the strings of lights back and forth across the branches."

"We can't decorate cuz the lights aren't done." Ellie looked at her forming her pout.

"That won't take long, but what we forgot are the old decorations." She motioned toward the hallway.

"Let's get the boxes, and the lights will be nearly finished."

Ellie's smile returned as they hurried down the hallway to the boxes. Josie gave Ellie the smallest one, and she managed it while she set the lighter box on top of the heavier one and lifted them both, grateful that ornaments weren't that heavy.

When she returned to the living room, Gramps and Chris were finishing the lights, so she and Ellie stood back waiting for the big reveal. In moments, Chris plugged them in, and Gramps stepped on the floor button that turned on the lights.

"Yeah!" Ellie bounced and clapped her hands, while Josie set the two boxes on the coffee table.

Chris stepped closer and put his arm around Josie's waist. "Finally, it's time to decorate."

She tried to force a laugh or even a smile, but she couldn't dismiss Ellie's drawing. She shifted closer to his ear, praying Ellie was so distracted she wouldn't notice. "Ellie drew a picture of her standing between her mom and dad. I'm sure she'll want to hang it on the tree or somewhere. Chris, it breaks my heart."

"She has to grieve, Josie. But I'm surprised. She's really never done that before. In fact, since she's been here, she's mention angels and heaven more than she ever has."

"She's older now, and maybe more aware. Christmas is family and love. That might have triggered it." Josie pulled back when Ellie looked their way and beckoned her to pick up some ornaments.

"Could be, but so far it hasn't dampened the tree decorating. She seems okay." Chris gave her a pat. "Let's focus on decorating. That will preoccupy her mind."

She touched his arm and squeezed. "You're right."

Following Ellie's signal, she headed to the table and pulled out two large Christmas balls. "Look at these, Ellie." She showed her the manger and on the other the Christmas star."

"Can I hang the star?"

"You sure can." She handed Ellie the star and hung the manger ball.

Gramps joined them, selecting a couple of ornaments and placing them high up where she and Ellie couldn't reach. Soon Chris joined in, and in time the boxes emptied until they had only a few novelty items like a chipmunk carrying a candle and two birds sitting on their bird house with a wreath over the door.

Ellie hung the last ornament and hurried to her side. "Can we get our decorations, Josie?"

"I think we can." She took Ellie's hand, and they darted off together to gather up the paper angels and her glittery paper stars before they collected the pinecone ornaments.

Ellie insisted on hanging hers first, and then she hung her two stars. When they carried in the pinecones, they shared them, except Chris came to their rescue to put two of them higher on the tree.

Josie stepped back, admiring their additions. "What do you think, Ellie? We did a good job, didn't we?"

"A really good job, but I have one more." Ellie swung around and darted from the room.

As Ellie disappeared, she arched her eyebrow and looked at Chris, aware that the drawing she'd done would be the final Christmas decoration. He glanced at the doorway over his shoulder and when he turned back, he shrugged. "She needs to hang it, Josie. Don't you think."

"Yes, but it makes me sad."

He frowned. "But I think it makes her happy."

Chris made a good point, and she nodded. "And that's the important thing."

"It is." As the words left his mouth, Ellie returned, carrying the picture that she'd colored and cut from the larger piece of paper. She'd found a piece of ribbon and had somehow attached it.

"I can put it right here." She walked to the front of the tree where a spot stood open, and she hung the ribbon over a branch. Her face glowed when she turned. "Do you like it?"

"It's lovely, Ellie." Chris shifted closer and put his arm around her shoulders. "Your mommy and daddy will like it too."

"I know. Cuz now you're my daddy and Josie is my mommy."

Josie froze hearing the child's explanation. "Ellie, is this me?" When she moved closer, she recognized Ellie's attempt to draw her features. Though distorted, she'd gotten the hair style right, and she'd captured Chris too. But it shouldn't have happened. Not her as the mommy.

"I love it, Ellie." Chris drew her closer and kissed her cheek. "You're a good artist, and you're the best daughter in the whole world."

"I am, Daddy?"

He pressed his lips together. "Thank you, sweetheart."

Gramps appeared on the sidelines, and eyed the two of them as if he wanted to say something but didn't.

When Ellie saw him, she motioned for him to come closer. "Look Gramps. Here's my family."

He eyed the drawings, and then turned to Chris and then Josie. "You made a lovely picture, Ellie, and they look just right."

She pointed again. "Daddy and Mommy." Her gaze shifted to Chris and to her.

She was at a loss for words, but not action. She had to do something to make things right and get ready to return home. The poor child had lost one Mommy. Before Ellie convinced herself that she'd found another mom, she had to leave.

Running out the door wouldn't work, so she stuck around for a while, and then made an excuse that she had to go back to the Inn. Chris gave her a strange look, but she managed to keep her emotions under control. "I'll see you later." She gave a friendly wave and left while a knife pierced her heart.

As soon as she returned, Rose spotted her with her face filled with questions. She talked around the problem and headed to her room. She had two days before Christmas and leaving now could stir up more problems than she wanted to handle. She needed a fresh plan.

After plumping her pillow, she flung herself on the bed and closed her eyes. Her mind spun with images and conversations, and though she longed to develop a plan, nothing fell into her mind that offered even the first step.

She closed her eyes, wishing away the images and turning the gears to her job and responsibilities at home. A buzz sounded in her head, and she opened her eyes and jerked herself up. Her ringtone. She eyed the time on her cell phone. She'd slept more than an hour.

The phone number looked unfamiliar, but she went ahead and hit the button. "Hello."

"Josie, this is Gramps."

Her back straightened. "Gramps? Is something wrong?"

"You tell me."

She pulled the phone away and eyed it as his meaning struck her. "Not wrong, but...maybe it is wrong, Gramps. I'm sorry but—"

"We need to talk, Josie. Can I come down there, or I could meet you somewhere?"

She checked the time and realized she was more than an hour late for lunch. "Mustang Lounge?"

"Great. We can have lunch."

"That's a good idea, Gramps." She wanted lunch and needed to speak with someone.

"What time, Josie?"

She gazed at her attire, aware she'd fallen asleep fully dressed. "Right now. I'm closer to the restaurant so I'll leave in a few minutes."

"See you there."

Josie clicked off, but sat still, sorting out what had happened and why Gramps had called. Her question had a built-in answer. He recognized the problem. Gramps' wisdom hung from him like a doctor's shingle. Gramps knew everything.

Maybe that's what she needed.

She shifted her legs to the mattress edge and lowered her feet to the floor. Her legs seemed weighted, but in truth, her mind carried the burden. She'd allowed her feelings for Ellie to be obvious, and she hadn't held back. Any child would make the assumptions that Ellie had made. She and Chris had been wrong allowing their emotions to be evident to even a child.

Eyeing herself in the mirror, she grasped a comb and ran it through her tangles. She looked sick, pale as the snow. But she didn't want to redo her makeup as she would have done for Chris. Instead, she dug into her purse for her lipstick. She smeared some lipstick along her cheek line and added a swipe to lips. She checked her efforts and saw it worked to brighten her face.

After slipping on her jacket, she hung her bag over her shoulder and left her room. Rose was busy in the kitchen from the sound, so she made her way to the street unnoticed. The temperature had dropped since the morning, and she hurried along aware that the heavy breeze had already undone her attempt to smooth her hair.

She turned the corner onto Astor and opened the Mustang Lounge door. She spotted Gramps already seated, his hand waving in the air. She gave him a nod and worked her way through the tables to him. When she stood in front of him, no words entered her mind. Trying to explain or even knowing what to say had escaped her.

Gramps rose and pulled out a chair adjacent to his. He eyed her a moment, but before either could say a word, the waitress arrived. She reviewed the menu, fearing she couldn't eat a thing but ordered a Rueben sandwich. She could always take it back to the Cottage Inn. Gramps placed his order, and the waitress left for their drinks.

Gramps waited and talked about the weather and everything but what she assumed he wanted to discuss.

When their drinks arrived, Gramps took a sip and then shook his head. "I know you're upset, Josie. You don't hide your feelings well."

"I know, Gramps. That's why I had to leave."

"Tell me your problem although I think I understand. It's about Ellie."

She gave a slight nod as tears blurred her eyes. "Did you see the picture she drew?"

"I did. Where you surprised that it was you and Chris in the drawing?"

"I thought it was her parents, and that made me so sad, but I felt worse when I realized she'd drawn Chris and me."

"Why?" He rested his hand on her arm propped on the table.

"You're a smart man, Gramps. You know the problem."

He leaned back, but his hand remained in place. "No. I really don't. You and Chris made friends fast, Josie. And you were both happy. I've never seen Chris so happy, and I mean that."

"He's a wonderful man, Gramps. I think so much of Chris."

"You do. That's obvious, and he feels the same, and here's what's confusing. You've been wonderful with Ellie, just like a mother or a special auntie. You do care about her."

A ragged breath tore from her chest. "I love her, Gramps, but I can't be her mommy."

"Why? If Chris hasn't proposed yet or at least let you know how he feels, then he's slower than I thought. It's obvious he's head over heels for you, Josie. And I thought you were the same. So why couldn't you be the mother that Ellie sees in you?"

"Because I can't get married."

He drew back, his hand moving with him. "You can't? Are you already married?"

"No. No. It's not that. I've vowed to never marry."

"You're a nun?"

Her upset couldn't stop her titter. "No, Gramps. I'm a single woman with no promises except to myself."

"If you're not a virgin, Josie, Chris will under—"

"Gramps, that's not the problem." Her mind tangled with her reason, a reason that had begun to frazzle since she'd met Chris. But she'd believed it for so many years. "Let me explain." She dragged in another floundering breath and told him about her two sisters' marriages, and the damage they had done to their lives and her one sister's children.

"Josie, have you said anything to Chris about this?"

"He asked if I had the same character and personality of my sisters."

"Do you?"

"No. We're different, but sometimes genetics play a part, and I don't want to ruin my life or Chris's and especially not Ellie's. She's already been through too much."

She barely finished the last word when the food order arrived. After the waitress refilled their beverages, Josie hoped the questions had ended. She studied her sandwich and wished she could eat it.

Gramps took a bite of his burger and set it back on the plate. "You eat now, Josie. I'll be quiet."

"I appreciate your concern, Gramps, and I'm not really hungry."

"I've made you upset." He looked at the table,

concern written across his face. "I'm sorry. I didn't mean to bring up things that upset you. I just wanted to—"

"To help. I understand." She bit her bottom lip for a moment, wishing she could explain how her mind worked, but she didn't understand it enough to explain.

"Hush now." He gestured toward her sandwich. "Please try to eat a little while it's warm."

She eyed the toasted marbled rye bread packed with corned beef, Swiss cheese and piled high with coleslaw. Maybe just a bite. She lifted the large sandwich and opened her mouth as wide as she could. The aroma drifted around her as she sank her teeth into the delicious sandwich. When she lowered the bread, her thoughts drifted to Chris and wondered what he was having for lunch.

Her chest ached when his image filled her mind. His dark hair, the color of Ellie's, stayed close to his head. She'd never seen it mussed even in the wind. And his smile had a toying almost shy playfulness that often haunted her dreams. His eyes captured her every time she looked at them, drawing her in to the mystery in the swirls of the deepest blue.

When she looked up, Gramps watched her as he ate, and she longed to run and not have to explain because she couldn't anymore. She didn't understand herself.

After two more bites, she returned the sandwich to the plate and would take it back to her room. Maybe later her appetite would return. "Gramps. I don't make sense, I know. Chris has told me how much he likes me, but he's never suggested making a commitment or making a reference to marriage. Nothing like that, and I fear that when we leave the island, Ellie will be heartbroken again."

Gramps leaned back and studied her a moment causing her to feel uncomfortable, but it was his way of thinking she guessed. Finally, he leaned forward on his elbows. "Josie, I would bet my life savings that Chris cares for you more than you know. I believe he loves you. He's talked to me about being comfortable with you more than any other woman he's ever met. He's looked excited when he says how great you are with Ellie, and how much she adores you. You must have known that without her drawing."

"I probably didn't see it since I adore her so much. It just felt natural."

"Yes, it is natural. There's nothing put on with you or with Ellie…or with Chris for that matter. You're all sincere about who and what you are to each other. I can't force you to give Chris a chance, but for Ellie's sake, I hope you will keep your plans to stay through Christmas. She will be devastated if you leave."

Devastated. Her stomach dropped to her knees with the thought. "I doubt if—"

"Trust me. She's been talking about Christmas and going to church with you, and the fun you'll have if another snow comes. She talks about snow angels and snowballs. She loves when you read her stories, and so many things that she says after you return home for the night."

"But I didn't know." Or did she?

"And it's not just Ellie. Chris mentions things that makes him laugh or smile, and ways you have that he likes or enjoys. You're the subject of many conversations at our house, Josie. Maybe I shouldn't tell you this, but you need to know."

Her head roiled with a mix of thoughts and images, ways in which Chris and Ellie had touched her life too. "Thank you for being honest, Gramps. You know I respect you so much. You're a wise man, and I'm honored to know you."

"Oh goodness, Josie. Don't be honored. I'm an old man bungling along with years of experience, and I suppose that helps with decision making and perception. But you're a wise woman too. Here's a thought. Sit down and make a list. Under each sister's name list the ways in which you are different. What got them into trouble in their marriages? And then ask yourself if you have the same problems. Can you handle things they can't? When you break it down, you might learn that the differences are too great to affect you."

"Make a list." She nodded. That's something she could do if she could be honest about herself. "I'll try, Gramps. I will do it."

"Good. I think you'll learn some important information if you do that. And meanwhile, please stay here until after Christmas. You'll make Ellie very happy as well as Chris, and you'll make an old man happy too."

She leaned over and kissed his cheek. "Thank you, Gramps."

"You're welcome, and by the way, I didn't tell Chris I was seeing you. He's been moping since you left, and Ellie's been whining about why you aren't there. I hope you can do something to cheer up the evening."

She grinned at him and his description. "I'll be over in a bit."

"Good. I believe Chris and you meeting in the restaurant as you did was meant to be, Josie. I do."

"So, do I. I just have a hard time admitting it."

Gramps grinned and took her hand in his as he leaned over and kissed her fingers. "Thanks for joining me for lunch."

"Thank you for asking, Gramps. I don't know what kind of mess I would have been if you hadn't called. I felt so lost."

"You'll never be lost. Not if I have any say so."

She gazed into the man's glinting eyes and couldn't help but agree.

Chapter 10

"Ellie, it's snowing." Chris motioned toward the window.

"Snowing?" She hurried to the window and pressed her nose against the pane. "Can we go out and play?"

He gazed at her eager face, his heart heavy. "We can. But we have to dress warm."

Ellie bounced as she often did before she came to a stop. "Where's Gramps?"

"He went out somewhere. Maybe to the store." He'd asked himself the same question. "Get moving, girl."

She giggled and darted down the hallway while he stood staring out the window, longing to know what happened with Josie. But standing there wouldn't answer his question. He trudged back to his bedroom to change. Anything to keep Ellie busy. She'd spent the morning asking about Josie, and he had no answers.

Before they left, Gramps appeared. "That snow is growing deep already. Did you see it?"

"We did, Gramps, and we're on our way out to

enjoy it." He gave a nod to Ellie who bounded from the hallway when she heard Gramps voice.

"Come with us, Gramps." She skipped to Gramps side and took his hand.

"Not today, Ellie. I slipped and slid back to the house already. But you two have fun."

"Okay." She beckoned to Chris, as he slipped on his snow boots.

"Where you going, Chris?" Gramps eyed his boots.

"Marquette Park, I suppose."

Gramps nodded. "Good choice. Lots of open space there."

Chris agreed, and when they stepped outside, Ellie let out a squeal. Gramps told the truth. The snow clung to the tree branches and piled along the sidewalks, growing by the minute. He turned down Market Street toward the Fort. The large park there with a huge sweep of grass made a great playground for snow angels, snowmen and snowball fights.

"Can we make another snowman?"

"Whatever you want, Sweetheart."

Ellie gazed up at him, that look in her eyes that he knew held a question. "Why can't Josie come with us?"

"I don't know, Ellie. Maybe she's busy today." His chest tightened as his disappointment grew. If he only understood what had happened, but he couldn't fix a problem he didn't know.

He changed the subject as best he could, and when they passed Cottage Inn, he distracted Ellie and looked the other way and pointed out the Fort Mackinac ahead.

Ellie picked up speed and he broadened his steps, clinging to her hand. When they crossed Fort Street, Ellie darted into the park and threw herself into a pile of snow, swinging her arms and legs to form a snow angel.

"Ellie, you're going to be too wet to stay out here. Let's not make snow angels today. Okay?"

Her chin dropped along with her downcast eyes, but the pout didn't appear. She pulled herself up not to disturb the angel embedded in the snow and turned to look at it. "I wish Josie could see my pretty angel."

"So, do I." He stepped away, wishing she would focus on a snowman or anything but Josie.

He turned away and scooped up a large handful of snow, formed it into a soft ball and tossed it at Ellie.

It hit her on the side, but some of the snow splattered into her face. Though she looked surprised she broke out in a giggle and reached down to grasp her own handful.

He stayed close, so she could be successful, and she was. The whole gob of snow whacked him in the side of the head and icy hunks sneaked beneath this collar. He tried to shake it off while Ellie laughed and formed another ball.

But before she finished, a snowball struck her back, and she swung around with a silly look at him while he still held his handful of snow. He joined Ellie pivoting behind him and his eyes widened as much as Ellie's as she yelled Josie's name. "You hit me."

Josie chuckled. "I did, and it was a surprise."

Ellie opened her arms and dashed toward Josie, slipping in the snow and standing again to reach her.

Josie leaned down and gave Ellie a hug. "I sneaked up on you, didn't I?"

"Yes, and I'm happy. I wanted you to come, too."

"I wanted to be here with you, too, Ellie." She crouched beside her and buried her face in Ellie's long dark hair tumbling from the jacket hood.

Chris stood back, confusion tangling with happiness. He'd wanted her there too. More than he would have believed a month ago. "How did you know we were here?"

She raised her head. "Gramps let me know."

"Gramps?" His confusion expanded to bewilderment. "I don't understand."

"Later, okay?" She shifted her gaze to Ellie.

He gave a quick nod. With her comment, he realized Gramps had called her. He pressed his lips together, irritated but then grateful. Gramps had a way that he had a difficult time understanding. He knew Gramps wasn't a mind-reader, but he had a knack...a wisdom to work magic. Maybe miracles.

With Josie there, Ellie become the little girl he knew. Her smile broadened, her eagerness to make a snowman returned, and her moping turned to happiness. Ellie became the four-year-old that wanted to have fun.

He became a man who faced the truth. He'd fallen in love and couldn't make it go away.

"Let's make a snowman." Ellie grasped Josie's hand and pulled her toward a clear patch of snow. As they packed the snow and rolled it, the ball became bigger and bigger, and he moved to another area and worked on the next snowball they would need for the snowman's chest.

Once they stopped, he rolled his compact ball to them, and then needed help hoisting it onto the one they'd made. Ellie joined Josie, and he grasped his side. "On the count of three." He called the numbers as they heaved the snow upward on three.

Ellie let go and danced around the partial snowman

until he and Josie couldn't contain their laughter. "Good job, Ellie." He gave her a high five.

Josie had already begun work on the snowman's head, so he beckoned to Ellie. "You know what we need. Two arms, a small nose and something to make the eyes." She bounded off toward the trees and shrub closer to the Fort and he followed.

When they returned, the head sat on the snowman's body, and Josie had already found two pieces of bark that she'd broken into two misshapen eyes. When they added the arms and nose, they cheered as he pulled his cell phone from his pocket.

"You two stand by the snowman and I'll take your picture." They posed beside the snowman and he snapped more than one photo to catch all the silly faces they provided. When he finished, the two gathered around the screen to see the photos and laugh at their antics.

The cold had gotten colder, and he eyed his watch and realized they'd been outside for close to two hours.

"I'm hungry." Ellie eyed him, and he'd already felt his own stomach growl. "It's almost five o'clock." He looked toward Josie. "Are you hungry?"

"Not starving, but I can eat."

"How about pizza? We can stop at Mustang Lounge, and I can call Gramps and see if he wants to join us."

"Pizza. Pizza." Ellie turned into a rubber ball again, bouncing around them in the snow.

He grinned but didn't comment. Instead he pressed Gramps number. "Want to join us for pizza, Gramps?"

"I think not. It's too cold. I just read the outdoor temperature. I'll manage here."

"We could bring some back, Gramps and you could heat it in the oven."

"Now there's a good thought."

Chris grinned, picturing his grandfather's face. "See you in an hour or so."

"That's fine. Have fun…and I'm guessing Josie is there with you."

"You're not guessing, Gramps. I already know."

"Ah, then you can thank me later."

Before he could add a rebuttal, Gramps hung up. He chuckled to himself, not wanting to say anything to Josie.

"Let's get a move on before we freeze in place."

"Then we could be like the snowman, Daddy."

His heart skipped. "We would be, Ellie, my girl." My daughter. The thought spun in his mind.

Josie glanced his way, but didn't respond. She stepped to his side, and Ellie squeezed between them, wanting to hold their hands. They made their way through the slippery snow to Market Street, hand in hand.

♥

Josie managed to hide the turmoil she'd struggled with since she'd become aware of how her life had changed since meeting Chris and Ellie. The child needed a mom, but she'd never planned to be one. The old saying, "the best laid plans of mice and men often go astray" rang in her head over and over.

And here she was again, holding Ellie's hand as they returned to Gramps from their pizza dinner. Though she'd planned to eat, the food lay stuck in her throat each time she looked into Chris's amazing eyes and Ellie's, that almost matched her uncle. She'd called him daddy again today, and in time, Daddy Chris would be long gone. Chris had become the little girl's daddy.

But what about a mommy? Chris needed to find a woman who could commit to a relationship, one who would marry him with open arms. If any man could be called "a catch," Chris was one. He had the finest attributes, the sweetest disposition, and the best looks of any man she'd ever known.

So what did she fear? Gramps had made a point. In what ways did she reflect her two sisters? She'd thought about a list, but hadn't made progress, even mentally. They had the same parents and that was about it. She'd been ridiculous to assume because their marriages failed that hers would too. Why had that thought entered her mind?

"You're quiet."

Her head jerked, hearing Chris's comment. "Sorry, I'm thinking. Christmas is very close, and that means heading back to the city."

He didn't respond.

"I've grown to love the small town feel of the Island."

All she saw again was a nod. "Now who's quiet?"

He shrugged but added a grin. "You reminded me how time has flown. They say it does when you're having fun."

Having fun. She had enjoyed herself more than she could say. "Thanks for dragging me along."

"No dragging, Josie. It was a great walk."

Chris's voice faded away, and his expression rent her heart. "It has been, Chris."

He gave her nothing but a look.

They turned onto French Lane, and in moments,

reached Gramps house. He waved her forward, and she climbed the porch steps and stopped at the door. Ellie slipped in front of her and before Chris joined them, Gramps opened the door. "Who's got my pizza?' He grinned.

"Chris, Gramps." She stepped out of the way as Chris moved closer and handed him the box. "It's probably frozen pizza by now." He grasped the door handle and pushed it open wider, motioning her to go inside.

Ellie darted past her, but Chris waited until she entered and then stepped inside.

Though not rude, Chris seemed distracted. The reason didn't need to be stated. She knew. Once again, they needed to talk. It filled her mind, and she suspected the same topic occupied Chris's.

Inside Gramps had vanished, and she could hear Ellie in the kitchen, piping away what she had done in the park while Gramps heated the pizza. Chris stood near the lighted Christmas tree. The handmade ornaments sparkled with the glitter they'd used, and the drawing Ellie had made of the family still hung, front and center. Her heart weighted with the child's open admission of wanting a mom, and she'd chosen Josie.

No way could Josie deny the love she felt for Ellie. The child had tangled around her heart strings and formed a love knot. If she didn't care, leaving would be easy, but it wasn't. Her mind shot back to the moment she'd heard from her friend Carol and faced the disappointment of not having company on the island. Yet she had the greatest company. Chris. Gramps. Ellie. Even Rose. Who would have expected a Christmas trip to change her life?

When Chris turned from the tree, he pointed toward the sofa. "Please have a seat." He headed that way, and when she sat, he sat beside her. She gazed at him, and he, at her, each with full hearts and minds, she knew. But noise from the kitchen warned them that this was not the time for serious conversation.

Within minutes, Ellie ambled into the room and sat on a nearby chair. She yawned and leaned her head back as if about to fall asleep. Chris glanced her way and then leaned forward. "Ellie, we've had a fun day. I think it's time for bed, don't you?"

She raised her head and sat looking his way. "Can Josie put me to bed?"

Chris's head jerked upward, then inched around to face Josie. He didn't ask, but she understood his look.

"I can put you to bed, Ellie." She rose and extended her arm toward the child. Ellie slipped off the chair and grasped her hand. "Will you read me a story?"

She glanced at Chris who gave her a slight nod. "I'd love to, Ellie."

"You can be my mommy." Ellie looked up at her as air drained from Josie's lungs.

"Pretend, right?"

Ellie frowned, then as if thinking it over, she finally nodded.

She waited a moment while Ellie got ready for bed, and then went into her room. Pretend mommy. The situation tore her heart. Ellie wasn't old enough to understand that being her mommy meant she would need to marry Chris, and she wasn't sure how Chris felt about that. She wasn't sure how she felt.

Ellie had a book picked out before Josie had a moment to think. She sat on the edge of the bed, leaning her back against the headboard, and began the story that Ellie had chosen. She began the story of a prince who longed to find the perfect woman to be his wife, but every woman he found had a flaw. Ellie loved the ladies flaws. One blew bubbles with bubble gum. Another wore two different shoes. The strangest one wore a veil over her face, and the most beautiful one only wore black dresses.

The characters made Ellie laugh, but as sleep weighted on her eyes, Ellie yawned, yet stared at her as if thinking. "You could be the prince's perfect lady."

Josie drew back. "I could?"

"Because you don't blow bubbles, you wear the same shoes, you don't wear a veil and you wear pretty colors."

"That's right, but I think there's more to falling in love."

"And you're pretty and nice, and Daddy Chris loves you."

"I'm not sure about that, Ellie. I try to be nice, but—"

"And you are pretty. Gramps thinks so, and I heard Daddy say it too."

"Well, thank you for telling me, but there's still more."

"I heard Daddy tell Gramps that he loved you. That's good."

Her words caught in her throat. Though she cleared it, she still choked on the words hanging there. "Yes, that's good."

A huge smile appeared on Ellie's face when she heard her response. "Then you can be my mommy."

Without further conversation, she leaned back on

the pillow and closed her eyes.

She sat there, watching the child until her chest rose and lowered in an even, slow rhythm. She eased off the bed, turned off the light, and waited a moment before leaving the room. Her mind reeled with the information Ellie had shared, and now she had to decide how to handle it.

Taking her time, she strolled down the hallway, wanting to stay goodnight, but certain that Chris would want to talk. The infamous talk that they'd referred to so often. An endless talk that had so many ups and down, edges and corners. Her head spun.

"There you are." Chris leaned forward when she stepped into the room. "I thought you fell asleep with Ellie."

"No, but it was a long story that had to be discussed, I learned."

"Discussed?" He tilted his head and waited.

"The prince was dealing with many strange princesses, but they all had flaws, and he wanted a perfect one."

Chris ginned. "Ah, and did he find her?"

"No, but Ellie did."

"Huh?"

"Did you know that I'm perfect for the prince?"

"No, but I could have guessed." He gave her a wink. "Ellie thinks you are perfect."

"The poor girl has no idea." She leaned back wanting to list all her flaws so he would ask her to leave and never darken his door, but he didn't let her.

"I think you're perfect, too, Josie."

"Oh, Chris, please—"

"We all have a few quirks. I'm sure you've spotted

mine, but those aren't who we are, Josie. We're the person that responds to the needs of a child, to the odd comments from a Gramps, and the confusing nature of the…prince."

"The first two are easy. I'm not sure about the prince." She managed a grin, but wished she'd kept her mouth closed.

"I'm not sure about him either, but what I'm sure of is that he's crazy about you, Josie, whether you want to hear this or not. You're right. Christmas is at hand, and we're both going to be on our way back to our lives in Birmingham and Royal Oak. But I said it before, Josie. Those two towns are on top of each other. What's a couple of miles?"

"It's not miles, Chris. It's me and my fears."

"Are you afraid of me? Do you think I'm lying to you?"

"No. No. Not at all. I have feelings too. I just don't trust them."

"Then we need to see what happens when we return home. Can't we do that?"

"Yes, but don't you see that Ellie has it in her mind that I'm her…"

"Her mommy. I know. Yes, I'm concerned." He paused and held up his hand. "Not that you wouldn't be a wonderful mom to Ellie. You've already proven that, but if you can't accept me. I'm not sure Ellie will understand."

"Yes, that's the problem, except it's not really you either, Chris. I accept you. I love who you are, and I respect you. You're an amazing dad to Ellie, and you're a wonderful grandson to Gramps. You're a hard worker. You're thoughtful. You're kind. And you're handsome. What woman wouldn't want all of those qualities?"

"You?"

"It's me, I don't trust, Chris. It's me."

"I don't understand, Josie. I really don't—"

"I don't either. I've told myself for years that I'm not marriage material, that I'm a loser as far as marriage goes. It's based on my sisters' failures. Not mine. But I can't get it out of my head."

"Let me try, Josie." He shifted closer to the next sofa cushion, slipped his arms around her back, and drew her to him. His lips lowered, touching hers with the tenderness of holding a newborn baby.

The kiss deepened as he eased her closer, his heart echoing a rhythm that matched her own. Her lungs failed her as a moan escaped her throat. She inched back, gasping for air and yet not wanting to leave the safety of his arms. Bound in his kiss, her problems and fears faded. At that moment, she could love him forever.

"Can you walk away from this, Josie? Can you dismiss the emotional pull that I know you feel, just as I do?"

"No. But I want to. Yet when you're here with me, I can't."

"Then the problem is gone. Can you look at it that way?"

"I'm working on it, Chris. I've been honest with you today, and I'm trying to understand why I assumed I would have my sisters' problems. I know it sounds ridiculous, but when a person gets a warped view of things, they seem real. I finally know that they are not. Gramps helped me so much."

His muscles tightened. "Gramps? I don't get it."

"Long story, but he called me, and we had lunch together. He's the reason I came today."

He drew back, his eyes wide. "You're kidding."

"No. It's the truth. He's a wise man, and he gave me some pertinent things to think about. I'm grateful that he called me."

"I'm startled, but I'm grateful too if it's helped you accept how I feel."

"I'm here. I might not have been, but he helped me sort and think."

"Good old Gramps." He looked down, his head swaying as if overwhelmed.

"I'll still need time, Chris, but I'm on the right path."

"I hope I'm on that path with you, Josie."

"You and Ellie. You're both there." She placed her hand on his. "Please be patient with me. I don't make rash decisions. I'm thoughtful. You know what I am since you've seen me in action...or lack of action."

He grinned. "But you acted this time, Josie. You've been here with us, and it's been an amazing time, and it's made a difference in my life and in Ellie's."

"And in mine, too. But we both must remember that it's only been weeks that we've known each other. Not months or years, but weeks."

"Weeks can be all we need. We're not kids. We've lived a stretch of life that has molded us and taught us about ourselves. We're both competent to make wise decisions."

"Are you convincing yourself or trying to convenience me?"

He grinned. "Validating." She lifted her hand and

cupped his cheek. "That's even better."

"It is." He leaned forward and brushed his lips on hers. "We don't need to rush into anything although I'd love to."

She studied his expression and smiled. "A little time. That's all I need."

He caressed her cheek, brushed his finger across her lips and paused while his eyes once again told her all she needed to know.

Chapter 11

The snow drifted past the window as Chris waited for Josie. Each day together made her more important in his life. The experience turned him on end at times. He'd never had that kind of feeling for any woman before, but she'd become a huge part of his life, and he'd grown to love it. Even planning involved her. She wanted to attend a Christmas Eve service, and he needed to check this evening's times of services at the churches. She hadn't mentioned which she preferred.

For some reason, Ellie wasn't underfoot as she had been the past two days since the gifts had been placed under the tree. He grinned at her feeble attempt to receive an early present. He'd thought enough to buy a stocking and stuff it with little items so she would have something to open on Christmas Day. He had a stocking when he was a kid, and he looked forward to receiving it and so did Ellie.

Before he could wonder where she was, he heard her strident voice sailing in from the kitchen. In moments, Ellie skipped into the living room, her gaze glued to the pile of gifts beneath the tree. "I'm helping Gramps make soup for lunch. I got to cut the vegetables—"

"Cut?" He nearly choked on the word. "With a knife?"

She giggled. "Yes, Daddy, how else could I cut?"

He eyed the kitchen door ready to march in and explain to Gramps that a four-year-old shouldn't use a knife. "I'd rather you not use a knife, Ellie. You could cut yourself."

Her grin faded to a frown. "No. Gramps gave me the knife we use at dinner."

"A butter knife?"

Her frown deepened. "I guess. It's not sharp but it cuts good."

Air drained from his lungs. "Okay, as long as it's that kind of knife." He stepped closer and gave her a hug, sorry he'd turned her smile into a frown.

"And I got to add the flavor things. That doesn't need a knife."

"That's right. Spices don't need a knife." He grinned at Ellie's expression, as if he were being silly.

She shook her head. "Not spices. Something else."

Rethinking, he deserved the silly look. "Herbs. That's what you added."

Her head bobbed like a galloping horse. "Gramps said the herds gave it taste."

"Herbs." He stressed the B.

She paused a moment and then sounded out the word. "Er-bs"

"Right." She made him smile now that she wanted to learn everything. "That's it. You got it."

Ellie had grown up since she'd come to the island.

He gave the credit to Josie who read to her and explained things with amazing patience. And that was from a woman who claimed she didn't have any.

Ellie's Cheshire Cat grin returned. "I'll ask Gramps and tell you when it's time to eat." She twirled around and skipped toward the kitchen, but when the door knocker sounded, she stopped, her face glowing. "Josie."

His heart skipped seeing the joy on Ellie's face. When the knob turned, Josie peaked inside. "It's snowing like mad."

"I saw." Heat in his face signaled he glowed too when he saw her.

Ellie changed her mind about the kitchen and rushed to the door. "Can we make a snowman?"

"Not tonight, Ellie." He beckoned Josie inside. "But if Josie doesn't come in soon, I fear she'll turn into a snowman."

Ellie tittered and shook her head. "But Josie has real arms that aren't sticks and a real nose and eyes."

"I noticed that." He met Josie in the middle of the room with an embrace that made him long for a life with her. Since their talk, he had allowed his feeling to come into the open. No more hiding or denying. He'd fallen hard.

So had Ellie, and she skipped across the room to Josie again and hugged her legs. Josie bent lower to return the hug. "How's, my sweet girl today?"

"Gramps said I'm a cook's helper."

"A helper. Wow, that's good."

"We made soup."

"Yummy." She took Ellie's hand and drew her across the room to an easy chair and lifted Ellie onto her lap. "What kind of soup?"

"With vegetables and stuff."

"Stuff. That's my favorite."

Ellie giggled and shook her head. "Me too."

Chris grinned at their silliness. "Do you remember what day this is, Ellie?"

She tilted her head as if thinking. "Is it Christmas?"

"It's Christmas Eve. That's the night before Christmas."

"Santa comes down through the chimney with gifts."

Josie gave him a subtle look. "He does, but it's also the night that Jesus was born."

She nodded. "And that's why Santa gives us presents."

"It is?" Chris gave Josie a sidelong look. "Why is that, Ellie?"

"Because the angels said the baby Jesus is our present, and then Santa gives us more presents, because he was happy about the baby born in a cow's house."

Chris clamped his jaw to avoid laughing. "It's called a stable."

"Stable." Ellie nodded. "And the wise people came and brought more gifts."

Chris's mind reeled with Ellie's explanation, and Josie seemed to have the same curiosity when she asked the question on his mind. "Sweetie, who told you this story?"

"Grandma Banks read me a book about Christmas. She said I could keep it, too."

"My mom." Chris nodded. "I should have known. When we were kids, she told us the story of Christmas many times so we wouldn't forget the true meaning."

"That's wonderful, Chris, and speaking of that, do you know what time the service is tonight?"

"Trinity Church starts at seven, if that works for you. That's early enough to take Ellie.

"Trinity is good." She shifted her attention to the Christmas tree and tilted her head toward the packages beneath. "Tonight or tomorrow?"

"After dinner or after church maybe."

Ellie squirmed off Josie's lap. "The presents?"

He and Josie couldn't contain their laughter. As she bounded to the tree, he captured her shoulder and drew her beside him. "Let's see if maybe we can open one present after lunch."

"I love you, Daddy." Ellie opened her arms wide and hugged him around the neck. His heart melted.

"Anyone hungry?" Gramps voice slipped through the moment of silence from the kitchen doorway. "It's ready."

Josie stood. "I'm starving, Gramps, so I'm coming." She joined Gramps in the kitchen as Chris lifted Ellie into his arms with a hug and followed. Today he would eat vegetable soup that Ellie helped make. His little girl—his daughter—had grown up.

♥

After lunch, Josie and Ellie cleaned the kitchen and put away the rest of the soup while Chris and Gramps went into the living room where she assumed Chris would pick out a gift for Ellie to open early. She'd been such a good girl.

When they finished and entered the living room, she spotted two gifts on the coffee table. Chris grinned and gave her a wink. Ellie saw nothing but the packages.

"Are these my presents?" Ellie stood beside the

gifts, her focus on Chris.

He nodded. "One's from me and the other's from Gramps."

She grasped the one with a strange shape and tore off the Christmas wrapping, finding a coloring book and large box of crayons. She grasped the book and hugged it before she turned the pages and studied the pictures.

Chris caught her attention and motioned to Gramps.

Her eyes brightened, and she darted to Gramps and planted a kiss on his cheek. "Thank you."

"You're welcome, Ellie. I'm glad you're here with me for Christmas."

Her head bobbed. "Me, too."

"The other gift is from me." Chris pointed to the gift bag.

Ellie dug into the tissue and pulled out a red pullover sweater with a delicate design in white. "Can I wear it today?" She held it up in front of her.

"If you'd like."

"I want to." She sank into Chris's arms and kissed his cheek.

Josie searched the packages under the tree and spotted her gift for the child. "You might as well open the gift from me, Ellie."

Ellie spun around, her eyes sparkling. "Which one, Josie?"

She rose and pulled the gift from under the stack and handed it to Ellie. She tore off the wrapping paper as her eyes widened followed by a squeal. "Yeah. A storybook."

Josie grinned. "Filled with fairytales."

Ellie opened her arms and rushed into Josie's.

"Thank you." She stood a moment, a shy look on her face. "Can we read it?"

Josie hugged her closer. "We can after we're done here."

Ellie hugged the book and then turned to the coloring book. "And we can color too."

"I think we can." Her chest tightened. In a couple of days, she would be back to work and home in Royal Oak while Ellie would be in Birmingham. An ache knotted her lungs. Life would be different.

She shifted her gaze to Chris. "We have a lot to fit in before I leave for home."

"Leave?" Ellie's face darkened, her eyes downcast. "You can't leave."

"I have to, Sweetheart. I go back to work soon, and my reservation ends at Cottage Inn." Smiles faded as if reality had become poison.

"I have an extra room here, Josie." Gramps voice cut through the thick silence." If you can stay through New Year's Day, why not?"

Why not? Because a child clung to her for needs she couldn't fulfill. Because a man turned her heart into a pinwheel, leaving her flustered and giddy. Because…

Three intent faces stared at her waiting for a response while her mind said one thing and her heart said another. "I need to get back, but thanks for the offer, Gramps."

Ellie let out a sob, her chin shook as the child looked at her with tears rolling down her cheeks.

"Ellie." Chris's tone gave a snap. "We all have to go home soon, so don't get upset."

Josie's heart ached looking at Ellie's longing look at her. Wanting to divert from her 'having to leave' comment, she suggested they color.

Ellie's sad face faded, though the cheerless look was still in her eyes, but she plopped on the carpet in front of the tree, and Josie joined her. They selected pictures and crayons while Chris sat nearby, his gaze shifting from her to the window and back.

Coloring helped occupy her mind, but Gramp's offer of a room at his house insisted on sneaking into her mind while she tried to select the blue and green shades she needed to create the picture. His offer had been kind, but too tempting.

She could stay on the island. Her work began after the new year, but staying only enticed her to consider what her heart longed for. Her emotions had no business getting involved. She'd always been a woman with a logical mind.

"That's a pretty picture, Jos..." Ellie turned to her own page, but her whisper floated into Josie's ear. "Mommy."

Chills ran up Josie's arms and down her spine. The child needed to understand before she was hurt. But as the thought struck her, realty struck her harder. The opportunity to avoid Ellie getting hurt had passed weeks ago. The damage had been done—to Ellie and to her. She adored the child, and Chris... Yes, she'd lost the battle.

The evening flew past in a flurry. Gramps loved his plaid flannel shirt and Chris wore his leather gloves to church. She'd saved one gift for Ellie to open on Christmas Day, a wise decision since Ellie fell asleep during the Christmas Eve service.

She gazed at the beautiful hand-crafted bracelet she'd received from Chris in shades of blue and lavender gem stones accented with silver beads. He couldn't have selected anything more lovely.

With Ellie in bed and Gramps heading that way, she knew that she and Chris would have time alone, time they needed to sort through the concerns she had. The Christmas lights reflected on the window, and on the other wall, the fireplace crackled with orange and yellow flames flickered against the dark backdrop.

When Chris returned from tucking in Ellie, he paused in the doorway of the hall. "You look beautiful, Josie. I don't know if I've ever told you that, but you are a lovely woman inside and out." He held up his hand as if he feared she speak. "I realize we've known each other for only weeks, but we've been through a lot during those weeks, and the things that happened during that time has made me feel more strongly about you."

She studied him as questions piled in her head. "Why are you saying this, Chris?"

"Because I want you to know how I feel." He ambled closer and stood beside the sofa.

"I'm learning that we feel pretty much the same, Chris, but I'm probably more concerned about the time element. We're here on the romantic Mackinac Island, the setting for starry-eyed movies and a place many people want as the setting for their weddings. I don't blame them. It's lovely here, but when we get back to reality, will all these feelings follow us?"

"I believe my feelings will, Josie." He stepped closer and settled on the sofa. "I don't play around with feelings. As you know, or maybe you don't, after I became guardian to Ellie, I haven't dated or even considered committing to anyone since I'm already committed to Ellie. I can't ask a woman to love me and also love a little girl, but—"

"But some women would love the little girl, Chris. How could they not? She's the dearest child, well-behaved, fun, appreciative. You've taught her well. Don't let that stop you from—"

"You forget that when we've talked, you admitted that you turned your back on love because of your two sisters' misfortune. We both have issues that don't always make sense to other people."

She squirmed with the comment. "Gramps talked with me about that, and you're right. He suggested I make a list of ways that I'm not like my sisters. I have more not likes than likes. Maybe because I was the youngest and they had each other until I came along. But I am different. They do things in competition with each other. I don't care what they do since I do what seems best for a situation. I've always tried to plan ahead and weigh choices. You know I'm not as adventurous as some people. Although I have to admit that—"

"You've certainly been adventurous here." He rose and drew her from the chair. "Josie, I want to give this a chance. My idea to devote all my time to Ellie is actually unfair and unreal. One day, she'll want her independence, and then I won't have a life. Plus, as you have seen, that sweet girl wants a mom, and I realize that I want a wife. Again, we've known each other only—"

"Chris, yes, only a short time, but—I can't believe I'm saying this—I want a chance to see what it all means too. Maybe when we return to everyday life our friendship will fade, but then, maybe not."

"Maybe it will grow." He drew her closer. "What do you think?" His mouth neared hers.

Thinking failed her while her chest fluttered like birds. She leaned into his waiting lips, his touch, warm and eager as hers. Her knees trembled as his hand glided up her back, his fingers brushing her hair and his mouth moving in caressing circles.

Her breath failed her, and when he drew back, they gasped as one. She rested her head on his shoulder, eyes closed, mind open to chances. She kissed his neck. "What I think is yes, I think it can grow. It will grow."

"Oh, Josie, I wanted to hear that. We have time to be certain, but then I'm already certain. I have never felt like this. Never."

She looked into his beautiful eyes. "I haven't either, Chris. Never."

"Then it's time to go home, Josie. Get our lives in order and give us a chance to test our conviction.

"It is time. I plan to leave the day after tomorrow. I don't want to leave the Island on Christmas Day, and Gramps has looked forward to our dinner together, but—"

"Yes. The next day is good. Ellie and I will leave too. I thought we'd stay a couple more days, but with you gone, I'd rather go home."

"Please don't change plans because of me, Chris."

He touched her cheek and turned her gaze to his. "Because of us, Josie. Us."

The word sizzled in her chest. Us. She hadn't known the meaning until now. Tonight, she felt the word in her heart.

"Us. I love the sound."

He leaned closer and touched her lips again, filling

her with warmth and hope.

♥

Chris broke the news to Gramps during breakfast. "We've had a great time, Gramps, and I won't leave you with all the decorations. We can take them down later—"

"Don't you even think of it. My neighbor Alice, the one who had her eyes on you for her granddaughter, always manages to come by a day after Christmas with a basket of goodies and the offer to help me take down decorations if I have any up. She's eager to help."

Chris broke into laughter. "Gramps, if this woman is a matchmaker, I think she has her eyes on more than me for her granddaughter."

"What do you mean?" A frown settled on his face but beneath it a silly grin could still be seen.

"Come on, Gramps. She comes with goodies and offers to help you. I think you have a woman who has her eye on you."

"Me?" Gramps leaned back and tried to slap his leg but he missed, and a silly look covered his face.

"You've already answered the question. Yep, one of these days…"

"One of these days what?" Gramps managed his deepest frown.

"We'll hear wedding bells. It's nice to have a companion. Someone to talk with and enjoy an evening together in front of the fireplace. Maybe read a novel together or share cooking a meal."

"Ah, Chris. I think you've got the wrong face near those wedding bells. I'm guessing we'll hear some mighty soon."

"Not too soon. But I won't deny it, Gramps. We had

a good talk, and we're both ready to give us a try."

"I'm glad, Chris. I'm happy for both of you, and for sweet Ellie. Josie is a good woman who doesn't think only of herself, but she's devoted to Ellie and to you. It's been evident from day one…or maybe day two."

Chris chuckled. "I didn't see it, but I don't want to think of life without her, Gramps. First time in my life I've said that, and I mean it. And you know that Ellie feels the same way."

"Same way?" Ellie bounded into the room from the hallway. "What's the same way, Daddy?"

No matter how often he'd heard her call him daddy, his heart always swelled. "You like a good breakfast."

"What is the breakfast?"

Gramps guffawed, and Chris shook his head. "What would you like?"

"Pancakes."

Gramps gave a nod. "Pancakes it is. Call Josie and see if she wants pancakes."

"Daddy, can I call and ask?"

"You sure can, sweetheart." He pulled out his cell phone, hit the speaker button, and then Josie's number.

Ellie grinned as she held the phone to her ear, and when her face lit up like a lantern, he would have known Josie answered even without hearing her voice.

"Do you want pancakes?"

"Hi Ellie. Are you making them?"

"Gramps is, but you can have some too, and then you can have a present I made for you."

"How can I pass that up, Ellie? I'll be there shortly so save me a seat."

"I will."

"Merry Christmas, Sweetie."

Merry Christmas, Mommy Josie." Ellie clicked off, her face glowing.

But Chris could only imagine Josie's reaction to Ellie's Merry Christmas. He had no idea how to stop Ellie from calling her mommy. She had been like a mother to her since she arrived, and Ellie needed that kind of attention. But he feared that pressure could cause Josie to question their relationship.

But how could he explain that to his little girl. He'd been dealing with a thought himself about Ellie's part in his life. He studied her and eyed Gramps who looked as if he was about to head in to make breakfast. Instead, he waited.

"Pancakes and I think we have some sausages too. And maple syrup." He rose and headed toward the kitchen.

Sounds good, Gramps. I'll be in shortly to help you."

"No need, Chris." Gramps stopped and turned to face him. "I've got it." He made a faint gesture toward Ellie. "I'm sure you two want a little time together." He turned back and vanished in the kitchen.

Chris sat down on the sofa and patted the seat beside him. "Come sit with me, Ellie."

She pulled herself away from the Christmas tree, eyeing a couple more packages that lay there. "Did Santa come to Gramps house?"

"I think he did. I see a couple gifts there that I don't recognize. Let's open them after breakfast when Josie is here."

Her smile grew bigger. "Okay, and Josie has another present for me, too. She told me."

He beckoned her again to sit beside him. "I want to

ask you something." He patted the seat again.

She tore herself from the tree and skipped across the floor to settle beside him. Her wide eyes gazed at him, melting his heart. He adored the child and hoped that she would understand what he had to say. "I want to ask you something that's a little confusing, but you're almost five now and I think you can understand."

"I'll be five on February ten."

"You will and then next year you'll start school. You're growing up too fast, Ellie."

"I don't know how to slow down, Daddy?"

He managed to laugh, but she'd said it again. Daddy. His heart had been telling him that they had to talk about that too. "Do you like to call me daddy, Ellie?"

She gave a big nod. "Because you are. My other daddy is in heaven, so you're my real daddy now."

"I love being your daddy, my sweet girl, but legally I'm your guardian, and that's different."

"But why do you have to be my garden when you should be my daddy?"

"Your real mommy and daddy asked me to be your guardian if anything ever happened to them, but no one thought that would ever happen, but it did."

She lowered her eyes and nodded. "I don't remember."

"It was a long time ago, so here's what I want to ask you. And if I confuse you, you ask me to say it again, okay?"

"Okay."

"If you want me to be your legal daddy, then we can go to court and instead of being your guardian, I can be your daddy. Ellie these are big words and ideas, but no matter what, I am being a kind of daddy to you, but this would make it legal. That means no one could say that I wasn't your daddy. I would be your real daddy on earth."

"I want you to be my daddy on earth. I don't want a garden."

"Guardian…but that's not important. If you want that, I can get a lawyer to help us make that come true."

She shifted to her knees and threw her arms around his neck. "Yes, I want you to be my real daddy now, and I want Josie to be my real mommy too."

He froze unable to think how to respond. Instead he tickled her and made her laugh while his mind spun with how to help her understand. He patted his lap. "Sit down and we can talk about that."

She dropped onto his lap with a kerplop and he chuckled, praying that the words would come. "You and I both like Josie and lot, don't we?"

"I love Josie. She's good to me and plays and we have fun. She makes me laugh and makes sure I'm being good. She's like a mommy."

"Yes, she's like one, but we have to use that big word again. Legal."

"I don't like that word cuz it's too had to understand."

"It is, but when you're born, for example, the hospital fills out a form with the name of your mommy and daddy on it, and the day you were born, and your name. Sometimes they put your foot prints on it or your hand prints. But that form makes you a legal part of their family."

Ellie's face sank into a frown, her eyes squinted but thoughtful. "And we need a form so that I can be legal."

"Right." He lifted his hand for a high five and she smacked it. "You got it. Now, the only way Josie can be your mommy is if she's on the form, but that means she and I have to be husband and wife, and we're not."

"Okay, but you can fill out a form to make you a husband and wife, and then she can be my mommy."

He stared at her a moment unable to know if he should laugh or cry. It sounded so easy. "That's right, but getting married needs to be planned and two people need to make sure that they will love each other their whole lives, so it takes a while for the form to be filled out."

"But you love Josie. I saw you kiss her, and you laugh and smile when you're with her so you love her, and then you can fill out the form."

"Oh, my goodness, Ellie. You have it all figured out." He gave her a hug. "Let me tell you what we're going to do. When we all get back home, Josie and I are going to spend time together and we're going to see if we are still smiling and kissing and laughing. If we do, then we will get the form and have a wedding, and she will be your legal mommy too."

"Yeah! Cuz I know she will laugh and smile and kiss you cuz you are so nice and good."

"Thank you, Sweetheart. You're nice and good too, and one day you'll find a man when you grow up who will make you laugh and smile and you'll marry him."

"And I'll kiss him too. Is that okay?"

"It's very okay." He kissed her cheek and held her close. "So as soon as we get back home, I will start working on the forms to make you my real daughter."

"I love you, Daddy." She hugged him tight and kissed his cheek. "Maybe I'll be your real daughter on my birthday."

"I hope it will be even sooner. Let's wait and see."

The doorbell rang, and the door opened with Josie peeking inside.

"Josie." Ellie jumped off his lap and darted across the room, her arms open wide. "I'm going to be on a form and Daddy will be my real daddy, and I'll be his real daughter."

"Wow, that sounds wonderful, Ellie."

"And then if you kiss Daddy and laugh and smile, you could be my mommy, but you need a form."

Her focus flew to Chris, but instead of looking upset, she grinned. "All it takes is kisses, laughter and smiles, and the form?"

"Yep. That's all it takes."

Josie bit her lip as if trying not to break into a full blown laugh. "I wondered how that worked, and now I know." She leaned down and gave Ellie a hug. "And since you told me that, I think it's time for your last present from me."

"A present." Ellie bounced and clapped her hands. She followed Josie to the tree and watched as she picked up a package and put it in Ellie's arms.

"You can open it now."

Ellie plopped on the floor, tore off the wrapping paper, and shook the box until the lid fell off. Along with the lid landed a plush kitten with a fluffy tail. "It's a kitty." She nestled it in her arms. "Can I name it?"

Josie knelt beside her. "You can, but first, look at her belly and push the little button you'll see there."

She turned over the toy and studied it a moment and then found the button. "Push?"

"Yep. One push."

Ellie pushed the button, and the kitten began to purr. "Listen, Daddy. It's purring. I think it's a girl kitty cuz she has a soft voice."

Chris rose and crouched beside her and Josie. "I can hear it. I think she's a girl. So what's a good girl's name for a kitten."

"Fluffy is good cuz she has a fluffy tail. Or Kitty. Or Mindy. She could have my mommy in heaven's name, and then she will be with me always."

Chris's chest tightened as Josie brushed tears from her eyes. "Pick the name you like best, sweetheart."

Josie gazed at him a moment and then turned to Ellie and petted the toy. "Mindy is a nice name, Ellie."

"My kitty's name is Mindy." She cradled the kitten like a baby, a smile filling her face. "Thank you for the present, Josie. I love the kitty."

"I thought you would like her and her purr."

Ellie giggled. "I'll show Gramps." She skipped away and in moments, Gramps let out a call that breakfast was ready.

Chris rose and helped Josie pull herself up from the floor. "Thank you for handling that."

"She'll have her mother close to her, Chris, and in a unique way. Ellie has been an amazing child to comprehend so much. In fact, I gather you're going to adopt her, Is that right?"

"It is. She wants it, and so do I."

"I'm glad. It's a wonderful idea, and since she was so young when they died, you've been the daddy she remembers."

"I know. That makes me sad that Gary didn't have the joy of raising her."

"But they know, Chris. I think they do know, and

they'll be with her in heaven as we all will."

He touched her cheek and guided his hand to her hair. "You're an amazing woman, Josie. I've told you that before."

"But you can keep telling me, Chris. I love to hear it."

He grinned and so did she. Smile, laugh and kiss. Ellie had everything figured out.

Chapter 12

Josie gazed at the calendar sitting on her desk. She had to return to work on Tuesday after New Year's Day. That gave her 2 more days of spare time. She leaned back in her desk chair as her mind slipped back to the day she left Mackinac Island. She'd done it with a smile, waving goodbye to Chris and Ellie who had cried when she said goodbye. And she had fought back tears since that day.

Ellie had gotten under her skin and flowed through her veins while Chris became the beat of her heart. But no matter how hard she tried, it all seemed so impossible. She'd seen Chris and Ellie one day since she'd returned. He'd called and invited her to lunch at Pronto's in Royal Oak. When he stopped to pick her up, her heart stood still as he came up the walk with Ellie bouncing at his side. When she opened the door, Ellie let out a squeal and hurried up the steps into her arms.

She turned into mush, like the snow she'd fallen into on the island. Chris said he liked her house. He sounded sincere. She loved the large living room with wide windows in the front and back so she could enjoy the flowering trees and bushes when they blossomed. The windows seemed to attract Chris too. He stood a while and watched the birds flitting on the branches and then flying to the bird feeders she'd hung filled with their favorite seeds.

When her cell phone rang, she jerked, not expecting a call, and when she looked at the caller's ID, she saw it was Chris. "Hi, what's up?"

"Ellie and I want to know if you can come over for dinner. We'll come over and get you so you don't have to drive here."

"I can drive, Chris, but..." But what? "If you're going out for some other reason too, that would be fine."

"I'll come by around four. Is that good?"

"That's early but I can be ready."

"Perfect. We'll be there. We miss you, Josie."

The words sent gooseflesh down her arms. She swallowed. "I miss you and Ellie, too, Chris."

"We'll work this out. I'm confident."

"Good. See you at four." She hit the off button and sat re-hearing his confident statement. Though she liked hearing Chris's confidence, hers lacked the same conviction. She still feared that one day something would happen, someone else would step into his life, and she would be forgotten.

She lowered her face into her hands and tried to force away her fears. If she could do life over again, she would want to ignore her sisters' failures and understand that she would build her own life and have her own opportunities to do it right. But she'd dwelled too much on their failure.

Ellie's image rose in her mind. A relationship with Chris belonged to him and Ellie as much as it involved her. Instead of worrying about herself, she needed to think of them as a trio—three people who had shared wonderful days and evening together on Mackinac Island. Why couldn't they enjoy the days and evenings in Royal Oak and Birmingham?

Determined to end her pessimism, she spent the afternoon, thinking of things they could do with Ellie. She lived close to the Detroit Zoo, and Ellie would love seeing all the animals—bears, giraffes, elephants, monkeys and so much more. A smile grew on her face with the thought. She'd heard of Java Jungle not too far away with fun slides and activities for children, and Kid City where children could play in a miniature city of buildings to stir their imaginations. She couldn't forget parks where Ellie could have fun on swings, slides and even monkey bars.

With some time to pass, she went into the kitchen and opened her favorite recipe book where she could find instructions to make some cookies. While she pictured Ellie helping her bake, she stirred the ingredients and baked them for Chris and Ellie.

Noticing the time, she finished the project and hurried into her bedroom. She wanted to look special and gazed in her closet for something Chris hadn't seen her wear on the island. She spotted her coral jacket and recalled a print blouse that highlighted the same hue. She pulled them from the closet along with a pair of black slacks, and changed into the outfit. The coral brightened her face, and when she added blush and lipstick with a similar coral tone, she grinned. For once she looked more like herself.

Off with the sad face.

Slipping on her last shoe, the doorbell rang, and she grasped her handbag and headed for the door. When she opened it, Chris stood behind Ellie who held a bouquet of flowers.

Josie stumbled backward and forced her gaping mouth to close. "Flowers?"

"For you, Josie." Ellie extended the bouquet toward her, and she bent down and hugged her as she accepted the flowers. "Come in." She stepped back to let them enter as she clutched the bouquet to her chest. "So what is the special occasion to give me flowers."

"Cuz we love you." Ellie's face glowed as she gazed up at her and then glanced at Chris.

Her heart in her throat, Josie bent down again and kissed Ellie's cheek. "And I love you too."

"And Daddy?"

She lifted her head, gazing into Chris's gorgeous eyes. "Yes, I love your daddy too."

"Yeah." She bounced in front of her while Josie gawked at the two of them more confused than she'd ever been.

"Let me put these in a vase." She motioned to the living room. "I'll be back in a minute."

The flowers were beautiful, a blend of carnations, lilies, and a smaller flower like an aster. She placed the bouquet next to the sink and dug out a tall white vase that had a border of green ivy that trailed down in spots. She pulled out the scissors and, as she snipped off the ends of the stems, she heard a sound behind her and spotted Ellie watching from the doorway.

"You can come in and watch, Ellie."

"Why are you cutting them?"

"It makes a fresh opening for the water to climb up the stem and keep the flower alive."

"Oh. Would they die?"

"Flowers die no matter what, but this helps them stay alive longer."

Ellie pulled a chair over to the counter and worked her way onto it and stood. Josie eyed her footing, worried she would slip and fall, but she didn't want to be overly protective either.

"Does everything die?"

The question dug into her chest. "Everything that is living has to die someday. But some things live for a long, long time, like trees, but flowers are more delicate so they have times to live and times to die, but their seeds can be planted again and then they will live again as a new flower."

"Like my mommy and daddy had to die, but they had a seed that was me."

"Sort of like that, yes. That's how all living things are made."

Ellie smiled at her with a look that announced another of her questions was on the way. "I'm a flower."

"You're a girl who is as pretty as a flower."

"I am?"

"You're beautiful, Ellie. One of the pretest young ladies I've ever seen."

"I look like Daddy."

"You do. You have the same hair and eye color, and you have his smile."

"That's cuz he's going to be my real daddy. He filled out the form."

"I know. And I'm excited about that."

"Are you going to fill out a form?"

She gripped the flower stem she'd begun to place in the vase and halted. A form? Her mind shot back to the form issue on the island. And now how to answer? "I haven't gotten a form yet, Ellie, but maybe one day, I'll—"

"One day you'll do the form. You need smiles, laughs and kisses, remember?"

"Yes, I do remember."

"Now you smile and laugh, so all you need are the kisses."

"What kisses?"

Chris's voice jarred Josie's blank stare, and she blinked. "Ellie's asking about my form."

He gave a quick nod and grinned. "We'll have to talk about that form, won't we?"

Josie pressed her lips together to stop herself from either laughing or crying. "I think we will."

Ellie seemed to have lost interest in the form and changed it to the flowers. She'd picked up the scissors without Josie noticing. Concerned, but not wanting to make an issue, she found an answer. "Ellie, can you please hand me the scissors."

Ellie looked at her a moment and then the scissors and relinquished them.

"I'd better get these in the vase before it's bedtime, or no one will have dinner tonight."

Chris moved closer and lifted Ellie from the chair. "Come on, helper, let's give Josie some room to finish the flowers." He put the chair back under the table and steered Ellie back into the living room while Josie placed the last bloom into the vase and cleaned the counter top. She carried the vase into the living room and placed it on a table to Ellie's delight.

"Now, I'm ready." She grasped her handbag again, slipped on her coat, and followed Ellie out the door with Chris behind her. From the look on his face, she knew another talk would happen about the form, and how they were going to get the idea out of Ellie's mind.

♥

Chris struggled through the evening whenever Ellie's references to the forms came up. She had a legitimate excitement about the adoption form. He'd completed it, and now they were waiting for the hearing. He'd been guaranteed that it would be no problem since he had been her legal guardian at the request of her deceased parents, and he was a relative and had been with Ellie for nearly three years. Still he would be relieved when it was complete, and the papers were signed.

Ellie preoccupied Josie much of the evening. He sat and watched them together and couldn't help but smile.

"Could I have that brown crayon over there, Ellie?" Josie extended her hand while Ellie located the brown color in the pile of crayons she'd collected next to her. Josie lowered her head and continued to color one of the pictures in Ellie's coloring book. His mind was on bedtime. He and Josie would finally be alone.

Ellie straightened and shoved some of the crayons back into the large box. "Josie, can you read me a story?"

Josie eyed her nearly completed picture before glancing at him. "If it's a short one, Sweetie, but I think it's getting late and your daddy has to drive me home before you go to bed."

"Do we have time, Daddy?" Her pleading look

made both of them grin.

"No, I think Josie is right. It's late sweetheart." He wanted to kick himself. How could he have forgotten that they would have no time alone tonight.

She gave him a pout that never worked on him, and after a couple of minutes, she gave up. "You go and get ready for bed, and then when we get back, you'll be ready. Okay?"

She lifted a shoulder as if she understood but didn't like the idea.

"Go ahead."

She did as he asked, and when she'd vanished down the hall, he turned to Josie. "I want to kick myself. I didn't think about not having alone time. I'm sorry."

"That happens with young ones, Chris. I understand."

"But I really wanted to…" He shook his head. "Never mind. I should hear in the next couple days when we'll have the hearing. I'm thrilled that it'll be finished, and she'll officially be my daughter."

"I'm so happy for you both, Chris. She wants that to happen, and we both understand that her real parents are so faint in her memory—"

"If at all. I've thought about that too."

Josie nodded. "You're the daddy she's known, and it will be a wonderful celebration."

"I can think of another wonderful celebration, Josie, and you know what that would be."

She nodded. "We still have time. You know I adore Ellie and I can't even explain how I feel about you."

"Could you answer this question?"

Concern covered her face. "What question?"

"Can you picture life without me?"

"I could only look back before I arrived on Mackinac Island, Chris. That was before I met you."

"But that doesn't answer my question. Can you picture life now without me in it?"

She studied him a moment, her lips pressed together, tension showing on her face.

His chest ached seeing her look, and it was too late to withdraw what he'd asked.

"I can picture it, Chris."

Blood froze in his veins, and he sat there like an ice sculpture.

"But I don't like that picture."

The ice cracked, and his back straightened.

"I can't lie, Chris. I would be lost without you beside me."

He rose and dashed to her side. "That's all I needed to hear, Josie. That's all I needed." His lips lowered to hers, and she leaned into his arms, her mouth as eager as his. The icy feeling melted with the flame of her arms around his neck and her lips on his.

"The kiss."

They jerked apart as Ellie's voice severed their embrace.

"Now you can sign the forms." Ellie bounded across the room and squeezed between them.

He looked at Josie, and they broke into laughter. Ellie giggled and grinned. She had all the steps she needed for them to sign the form.

What would life have been like without this amazing little girl? He bowed his head and thanked his brother and sister-in-law for the gift of being Ellie's guardian and soon her daddy.

♥

Josie slipped on her dress and eyed herself in the mirror. New Year's Eve had arrived faster than she imagined, and the time spent with Chris and Ellie had continued to be wonderful. She couldn't believe that a sad situation with her friend Carol had been the beginning of her relationship with Chris and Ellie, giving her a new life. When she called Carol earlier, she was thrilled to hear that her son was now fine and all was well. And yet she and Carol had missed the good time they'd expected to have on Mackinac Island.

Yet, another experience greeted her, one she would have never imagined. She met Chris because of her jacket falling on the restaurant floor. Her head still spun with that memory.

She turned in the mirror and added a necklace that picked up the color of the dress and a pair of matching earrings. She'd selected shoes with lower heels since Chris had mentioned music and dancing. With a new year beginning, she wanted it to be a memorable evening without tired feet.

When the doorbell rang, her heart skipped, and she hurried to the door and opened it. Chris grinned with a small bouquet of flowers, looking handsome in a dark suit and subdued tie. She rarely saw him in a suit, and it was always an amazing surprise when she again acknowledged how handsome he was.

"Come in before you freeze." She stepped aside, and he entered and opened his arms to her. She stepped into his embrace as his lips met hers without hesitation. The kisses she had longed for, and still did, had become a natural part of his greeting. She remembered times, after their first kiss, that she yearned for more and wondered how she'd gotten through life without the sustenance of such wonderful experiences.

"The flowers are lovely, Chris. You spoil me."

"It's Ellie. She made me promise to bring you flowers." He winked. "And letting her help me pick them out was the way I got her to agree to stay with my parents tonight so that I didn't have to worry about getting home."

"You mean you can be a big boy and stay up until midnight."

He chuckled. "Something like that."

She hurried into the kitchen to find a vase, and this time, she didn't trim the stems. She could do that later. She returned to the living room with the vase and bouquet, set it on the coffee table and stood back to admire it. "If Ellie helped select it, she did a good job. That's a lovely bouquet."

The white and pale pink flowers were highlighted with silver wash on the green leaves and silver ribbons. "They sing out Happy New Year, don't you think?"

He gave a nod combined with a shrug. "I think Ellie liked the silver color because it glittered."

"She does love glitter." She studied him a moment. "Are you ready to go?"

"Yes, but I can't stop staring at you. You look amazing."

"So do you, but I doubt you want to stand here all night and look at each other."

"No, I bought the tickets to Strada. We might as well use them."

"Strada? That's pretty fancy." She'd never been there but heard it was very nice.

"You're worth it."

She gave him a teasing poke, picked up her coat and

evening bag and motioned to the door. "If the chariot awaits, we should go then."

He gave her a princely bow, and she chuckled as they headed out the door.

Strada wasn't too far from her home, and after he parked, they walked hand in hand to the entrance on Main Street. Music from inside reached the doorway. They entered and were led to their table, along a side wall with less traffic. The menu included a meal of short ribs, Italian sausage and peppers, and endive lobster salad. They studied the choices and were overwhelmed.

"This is wonderful, Chris. I've never been to an evening like this for New Year's Eve. If I did anything it was a house party or just a quiet evening watching the ball drop in New York City."

"Many places show that on TV at midnight. Maybe you won't miss it."

She grinned and shook her head. "You're always so thoughtful."

He chuckled at her and then rose and extended his hand. "Dance?"

The music had slowed, and she rose, looking forward to swaying in his arms to the rhythm of the music.

Chris held her close as they moved around the dance floor. When he twirled her around, she caught her breath, loving the feeling of his strength holding her safe. He drew her closer again, and she felt the beat of his heart against hers. He looked into her eyes and sent her emotions soaring. She had no decision to make about a commitment. She'd been committed long ago even though she tried to deny it.

His smile warmed her, and when the song picked up the beat, they joined in, laughing as they twirled and moved along with other dancers, but when they both tired, he gave a head nod to their chairs and she agreed. When they returned, stemware had been added to the table, and they suspected a midnight toast was coming.

Josie glanced at her watch, surprised to see the hour hand so close to midnight. "The evening has flown by."

"It has, and before it ends, I want to talk about a couple of things."

A chill ran up her back. The look on his face seemed strained, and it suggested that the topic was sensitive. Was this a goodbye?

"You and I have been quite open about our feelings lately. Do you agree?"

She gave him a nod. "I'm surprised, but yes, I agree."

"We still have time, Josie. A commitment doesn't mean everything happens tomorrow. It means that when we're ready, then we can make a move."

"I know we have time. No matter how we feel we haven't known each other long."

He lowered his eyes to the table. "But you did say that you can't picture life without us being together. Right?"

"You know that's what I said. Each day that passes I believe what I said even stronger. You've become part of my life, Chris. You and Ellie."

"Okay, we're on the same path then."

She grinned. "I guess you could call it that."

He eyed his watch before lifting his eyes to hers. "Then before midnight, I want to ask you something."

"Okay." Although she'd thought he'd asked her

everything. She waited.

He reached into his pocket as he grasped her hand with his free one. "Tonight is the end of the year and the beginning of a new year. We're about to begin a new year together, and so I wanted to ask you, Josie, if…" He placed a small box on the table in front of her. "If you'll be my wife and Ellie's mother."

A gasp shot from her lungs as she gazed down at the box. "Chris, you're proposing to me."

"I am. We're not talking wedding tonight. We're talking the promise of a wedding whenever you're ready." He lifted the box and held it in front of her. "I told Ellie before I dropped her off at her grandparents that we were going to talk about the form tonight."

"The form." She couldn't help but smile. "I don't want to disappoint that sweet girl."

He extended the box again and this time lifted the lid.

She lowered her gaze to the gorgeous solitaire diamond that shot fire in the dimmed light. "Chris, it's beautiful. I've never seen one that brilliant."

"Only the best for my future wife, a woman that I fell in love with the day I picked up her jacket."

"No, you didn't."

"Close. You intrigued me that day, and I couldn't get you out of my mind. My pulse skipped when I saw you again, and I knew it meant something. As days went on, and when you encouraged me to bring Ellie to the island, I knew why I felt as I did. You were a woman with a huge heart filled with love and generosity, and an amazing spirit that I'd never experienced. I knew that I couldn't let you get away."

"I liked you from 'Is this your jacket?'"

Chris shifted his chair closer to hers and lifted the ring from its bed and held it out to her. "Josie, will you be my wife. I promise to love you forever."

"I can't pass up that kind of commitment, Mr. Banks. Yes. Yes. Yes." He slipped the ring on her finger and leaned across the table, pressing his lips to hers. When he drew back, his eyes captured hers. "I love you, Josie, with all my heart and soul. I believe this love was meant to be."

"I love you, too, Chris, and you know I adore Ellie. I agree. I sensed our meeting was part of our life plan. It always felt right even when I tried to make it go away because of my foolishness."

"We were both foolish, but even that got sorted out to make things good." He grasped her left hand and gazed at the ring on her finger. "It looks even more beautiful on your hand, Josie. Do you have any thoughts about the wedding? I'm not rushing you, but—"

"Don't apologize, and you're not rushing me. I've already thought about it. So often, Chris. Could we get married in June or July on Mackinac Island? It's where it all began, and I would love to begin the next chapter of our life in the same place. There's the Old Stone Church where we could have the wedding and then we're not far from the Grand Hotel, and that would make a lovely place for a honeymoon."

"You read my mind, my love. That's the perfect spot."

"I can't wait to tell Ellie." She gazed at the ring glinting as her hand lay in his.

"She'll be ecstatic. A Daddy and a Mommy. It's what she's always wanted."

"I know, and I'm happy that I'm the mommy she'll get."

"So am I, my love. So am I."

When the crowd began to count, Chris rose, drawing her from the chair, and they both joined in. "Five. Four. Three. Two. One. Happy New Year."

The words echoed throughout the restaurant as people cheered and hugged their friends, but Josie didn't care. She was in the arms of the man she adored. "I'm so happy, Chris. You've made my life so different and so wonderful."

"It's a new year and soon a new life for us. And I know, Josie, that it will be even more wonderful. We have a lifetime."

"We do, and I'm grateful that you didn't give up on me."

"How could I? I adored you."

His lips met hers, tender yet amazing. They had a lifetime to share, and she couldn't wait to be Ellie's Mommy and Chris's wife.

Mackinac Island in June

Josie stood on her balcony at the Grand Hotel dressed in her white wedding gown and looked down Cadette Avenue all the way to Market street with the line of old fashion lamp posts along the way. The hotel's green lawn and flower gardens washed in color added beauty to the scene. And down the avenue, she could see the Little Stone Church with its white steeple and stained-glass windows where she and Chris would be married.

She couldn't believe the June day had finally come, and she longed to see Chris who'd spent the night at Gramps with his parents and Ellie, now Chris's legal daughter, who couldn't wait to be the flower girl.

A carriage headed up Cadette Avenue toward the hotel decorated with white flowers, and her heart skipped, guessing it was the carriage that would take her and her parents to the church. She stepped back inside the room, a room she would share with Chris that evening, and admired the lovely décor. Using the hotel's geranium motif, the room was decorated with a pink geranium design displayed with green leaves on the white wardrobe and furniture, and a flowered canopy hung above the bed with the same pink geranium design.

A knock at the door sent prickles up her spine. She opened it to greet her mother dressed in a pretty lavender gown and father in his dark suit and tie. She opened her arms and hugged them as they entered, each gazing at her as if they had never seen her before.

"You look beautiful, Josie." Her mom brushed tears from her eyes, while her dad fiddled with his tie.

"You both look great, too. I love your dress, Mom, and Dad, I so rarely see you in a suit. You're a handsome man."

He grinned and stuck his hands in his pockets as if he didn't know what to do with them. "I think the carriage is out there, Josie. We should probably get to the church."

She glanced at the clock. "We can't be early though. Chris has to be there first so he doesn't see me."

"Your sister called and said they were there already."

"Both of them?"

"Audrey and Carrie came together. They're staying at the Inn that you stayed at in the winter. Someone named Rose was happy to hear you and Chris are getting married."

"She's the Innkeeper. Such a nice woman. I should have invited her, but…"

Her dad shook his head. "You wanted the wedding small so we didn't invite everyone who wanted to be here."

She lowered her head, recalling the battle she fought to keep the wedding intimate. She and Chris both wanted a celebration of the people who were dearest. "Maybe one day, we'll have a big twenty-fifth anniversary party."

Her mom grinned. "I hope I'm still around for that,

Josie."

"So do I, Mom, and I think you will be."

Her cell phone rang, and she jumped. "Who could that be?" She glanced at the number and it hit her. "Gramps." She smiled and answered. "Okay, Gramps. We're leaving now."

She ended the call, her heart beating out of her chest. "Everyone's there."

Her dad slipped his arm around her and guided her through the door while her mother made sure it was locked and hurried to catch up.

As she walked through the lobby, she smiled at the many people who gazed at her, some with silent applause and others with a big grin.

The carriage she'd seen was waiting, and the driver helped her and her parents into the cab. The clop of horse-hooves she'd heard in the winter again sounded along with the jingle of bells. Her heart sang as they neared the Little Stone Church. Once they'd alighted, she waited while a groomsman escorted her mother down the aisle to her seat.

Josie loved when Chris said his brother and one of his best friends would serve as his groomsmen. She'd also taken a big step and asked her two sisters to serve as her bridesmaids. They had both agreed, and somehow the invitation had eased the stress she'd felt with them all those years.

She could imagine Ellie bouncing somewhere in the church as she waited to sprinkle flower petals along the way. Her good friend Carol, who had missed the island trip in the winter, was there with little Jacob who was now a healthy three years old and serving as the ring bearer.

She and her dad neared the doorway, and when the sound of the Trumpet Voluntary began, her father linked his arm with hers, and they entered the church. The groomsmen and bridesmaids were at the front already. Ellie ran to her, and Josie bent down and kissed her cheek, then motioned for her to start down the aisle. She looked darling in her pink dress with a darker pink and white flowered border. She carried a basket with pink ribbons and filled with pink rose petals.

Next Carol shooed little Jacob to follow Ellie, and since he seemed to like her, he hurried on down the aisle without a problem. Everyone rose when Jacob arrived at the front, but Josie's eyes were on Chris. Her heart swelled as she drew closer on her father's arm, so glad he was there to keep her from falling to the floor with her knees weakening with each step. She'd never dreamed of this day, and yet, here she was.

Chris's face glowed, and tears blurred her eyes to see the joy in his face, and know the joy in her heart. They were meant to be as one, and today was the day.

When her father said the words that gave her away, Chris's hand became her strength. They faced the reverend, listening to the words that would bind them together forever, a journey that she had longed for since she admitted that she loved him more than herself.

They spoke the vows, and their "I dos" made them smile. The pastor prayed, and the rings were exchanged while she held her breath to hear him say, "You may now kiss the bride."

Chris's lips met hers in his tender, sweet way that sent her heart soaring to heaven. When she looked into his amazing eyes, she heard the words. "Let me be the first to introduce Mr. and Mrs. Christopher Banks."

All those present applauded and cheered as she and Chris headed down the aisle to greet their guests and to ride the carriage back to the Grand Hotel where they would have an amazing meal. Today she would sit beside the man she loved, her husband and best friend, and her little daughter Ellie. Tears filled her eyes, but she sent up a thank you to heaven. Her journey had just begun and she looked forward to every step.

♥

Chris rose from the table, pleased with the wonderful meal they had selected at the Grand Hotel, and even more grateful that Josie had agreed to be his wife. Even when he attempted to be social, he found his gaze shifting to her, looking gorgeous in the lovely gown that clung to her hips but swirled at her feet. She wore a tiara of flowers in her hair as did Ellie, and when she looked at the child, he could actually see features of Josie in her face.

He recalled one day when a store clerk looked at the three of them in Birmingham and said they had no doubt that Ellie was their daughter. They only smiled and didn't explain the truth. Today Ellie was their daughter, and from day one of seeing Josie with Ellie, he had no question that she would be the best mother in the world for his little girl.

"Are you ready to visit the guests?"

Josie smiled and pushed back her plate that still contained some of the prime rib and twice baked potatoes. Dessert had just begun to be served, and he suspected that, with the quantity of the dinner, many would decline the dark chocolate mousse cake or the lemon-lime cheese cake.

"Ready or not, here I come." Josie chuckled and

rose. He suspected she'd tired as he had. He slipped his arm around her back as they moved among the family and few friends to thank them all for being part of their special day. Ellie had decided to cuddle close to Gramps. She'd worn herself out with all the bouncing and excitement that had gone on the past couple of days with so much company and meeting her new maternal grandparents.

Though he'd heard a lot about Josie's dad, he liked the man, a hard worker who enjoyed his work and loved his family. As he'd studied her mother, he saw the resemblance and guessed that she'd been a beauty too. Meeting Josie's sisters, Audrey and Carrie, had been interesting having learned so much about them, but he watched their interaction and suspected that time had changed Josie and her sisters since today sisterly love shown as brightly as the sun, and Aubrey's children were well behaved and get along well with Ellie.

Little by little, people rose stretching their arms and coming toward them to say goodbye. A few were staying at the Grand Hotel, but many had chosen a hotel on Main Street, and his parents and Ellie plus his brother were staying with Gramps.

As they left, he and Josie stood near the doorway to say goodbye, and when the last few hung on, he decided to end the evening and head upstairs. His heart skipped each time, he looked at Josie.

"Are you ready to go up?" He watched her expression and was happy to see that she was ready too.

"Let's make a quick circle around to say goodnight, and naturally, we'll see some of them tomorrow anyway."

"True." He slipped his hand into hers, as they passed among those who remained. Each repeated their congratulations, and a few sent them with other kind thoughts. But all he could think of was spending time with Josie. Alone.

Ellie had been the hardest to leave. She begged to stay with them at the hotel, but Josie finally took her aside and said something that quieted her. He longed to find out what she'd said.

They rode the elevator up, and she guided him to the room that he had yet to see. When he opened the door, he understood her excited comments about the room. It had a delicacy that Josie would love and offered the bonus of a balcony that looked out over the island. For fun, he lifted Josie in his arms and carried her inside. She squealed and clung to his neck, but when he set her down, her kiss made the squeal worthwhile.

"It's a great room, Josie. I see why you like it."

She grasped his hand and pulled him forward. "Look outside." They walked to the sliding door and stepped out to the balcony. Ahead he could see the lights coming up on Main Street and the lamp posts lit along Cadette Avenue. Ahead in the dusky light, he spotted the Little Stone Church where he and Josie had promised to love each other until death parted them. He believed he would love her beyond death.

"It's a great view."

"It is. I love watching the carriages come up Cadette. You can hear the clop of their hooves and sometimes catch a jingle of bells. It reminds me of Christmas and the hayrides."

He touched her soft cheek and turned her face to

his. "And the kisses." He lowered his mouth to hers, and tonight, the kiss connected them in a new and amazing way. He deepened the kiss, and a groan escaped her throat. His body trembled with the depth of love he felt for her, and she grasped his back and drew him closer, closer than he'd ever been, as if they had become one. Tonight opened new doors and new dreams. His memory swept back to the day they met, and even then something happened as they talked. He sensed their meeting had not been a coincidence but a meant-to-be moment.

"I'm thinking of that first day at Mustang Lounge. Remember."

"I do."

The two words swept through his body. "I love you, Josie, beyond words."

"I love you too, Chris. You and Ellie." She lifted her eyes to his. "I do."

"I do, too, Josie. You and Ellie are my world." He paused as his question rose. "By the way, what did you say to Ellie tonight to get her to leave without crying?"

She grinned. "That should be my secret, but I guess since you're my husband I can share it."

"Please."

"I told her we had some other forms to talk about and we needed to be alone. When she asked what forms, I said, maybe she might like a brother or sister one day, and you and I hadn't talked about that yet."

"You did?"

"I did. And she was thrilled. She said please talk and sign the forms. So tonight, we need to talk about that."

"I don't think talk is necessary, my love."

She gave him a crooked grin, and he held her close, confident that life would be amazing.

Their lips met again, full and sweet and ready to start their new life together. The Bible said something about two are better than one, but today, he knew that three was better than one, and maybe even four. Now he knew for sure that Ellie would love to be a big sister.

He gazed into Josie's eyes, seeing that she too was ready for their life together. He eased back, his chest tight, his heartbeat strong as he gazed at Josie's beautiful face, his love ready and waiting.

The End

Keep reading for the first chapter of Lost in Red Rock Country

Dear Friends,

I love Mackinac Island in the Straits of Mackinac between Michigan's Upper and Lower Peninsulas. The island community is like stepping back in time with no motorized vehicles and a lifestyle that depends on ferries, frozen ice or airplanes to take them to the mainland. I wanted to share the life of this town during the winter months, and what time can be better than the Christmas season. I hope you enjoyed the book and the characters, especially Gramps and Ellie.

I would love to hear your comments via Amazon.com which allows you to rank the book and leave your thoughts. These comments are the best form of promotion for the author.

If you enjoyed Mackinac Island and haven't read my novella, here is a link that will take you to the purchase page so you can read the book description. Click here: True Riches.

I also want to share the Potato and Corn Chowder recipe found in the novel. It's excellent and easy to make.

Thanks for being a reader and a friend.

Gail

Corn and Potato Chowder

Ingredients:
1 30oz. bag of frozen diced hash browns
1 32 oz box of chicken broth...

4 large potatos, diced
1 can of cream of chicken soup (10 oz)

1 can of whole kernel corn

1 can of cream style corn
1 pkg. cream cheese (8 oz, not fat free)
5 pieces of crispy fried bacon broken into bits or 3 oz bacon
bits
1 cup shredded cheddar cheese
salt and pepper to taste

Directions:
Put the potatoes in the crockpot. Add in the chicken broth,
cream of chicken soup, both cans of corn, and half of the
bacon bits. Add a pinch of salt and pepper.
Cook on low for 8 hours or until potatoes are tender.
An hour before serving, cut the cream cheese into small
cubes. Place the cubes in the crock pot. Mix a few times
throughout the hour before serving.
Once the cream cheese is completely mixed in, it's ready to
serve.
Top with cheddar cheese and some additional bacon bits.

Best-selling and award-winning novelist, Gail Gaymer Martin is the author of contemporary romance and romantic suspense with 77 published novels and over four million books sold. Her novels have won numerous national awards, including: the ACFW Carol Award, RT Reviewer's Choice Award and Booksellers Best. CBS local news listed Gail as one of the four best writers in the Detroit area. Gail is the author of Writer Digest's *Writing the Christian Romance.* She is a founder of American Christian Fiction Writers and a member of Advanced Speakers and Writers. Gail is a keynote speaker at churches, civic and business organizations and a workshop presenter at conferences across the U.S. She lives with husband Bob in Sedona, AZ. Contact her by mail at: PO Box 20054, Sedona, AZ 86341 or on her website or social media.

Website:www.gailgaymermartin.com

Facebook: www.facebook.com/gail.g.martin.3

Twitter: http://twitter.com/GailGMartin

GoodReads: http://bit.ly/1e8Gt6D

LinkedIn: www.linkedin.com/in/gailgaymermartin

Novels - *Reissues*

Dreaming of Castles 2014

Novels - New

Treasures Of Her Heart 2014

Romance By Design 2015

Novellas   Reissues

An Open Door

Apples Of His Eye

Better To See You

Once A Stranger

Then Came Darkness

To Keep Me Warm

True Riches

Yuletide Treasures

Over Her Head

Love Comes To Butterfly Tree Inn

A Love Unforeseen

Novellas - New

Lattes and Love Songs 2015

Apple Blossom Daze 2016

A Trip To Remember 2016

A Tucumcari Christmas 2016

Poppy Fields and You, March 2017

Love Comes to Butterfly Tree Inn March 2017

Tumbling Into Love May 30, 2017

Lost In Red Rock Country Sept, 2017

Anthology Titles

Christmas Potpourri

Forget Me Not Romance #1

Love Blooms In The Here & Now

Mocha Marriage

Romance Across the Globe

Romance On The Run

Seven Mysterious Ladies

With This Ring

A Kiss is Still a Kiss

Get Your Kiss On Route 66

Valentine Matchmakers

All Mixed Up

Love In Danger

California

Second Change At Love

When Love Calls

The Hope of Christmas

Happily Ever After

Romancing The Wild

Returning Home

Coming Home Again

Read the first chapter of Gail's recent release: **Lost In Red Rock Country**

Chapter 1

Willow sat on a rock and looked out across the amazing landscape. Red Rocks appeared in every direction, formed into shapes from the wind and rain. They depicted everything an imagination could find and many were named from those well-known images—bell, submarine, coffeepot, cockscomb, castle, cathedral, Madonna and Child, and the one everyone loves, Snoopy Rock.

She dug into her hiking bag and pulled out her camera. Though she'd taken pictures of the rocks often, the sunlight, clouds and shadows, created new images, depending on the weather and time of day. Today a golden light struck Bell Rock and Courthouse Butte as if coated in gold.

Living in Sedona had been a kind of gift from her dear aunt and sadly her mother, in a way, when she became too ill to handle her arts and crafts store. The memories circled in her mind, and thoughts of her life before the red rock country had grown pale in comparison.

After she returned her camera to the bag, she rose,

having caught her breath from the arduous climb she'd managed. The rugged landscape beckoned to her and headed deeper onto the mesa. Wild Horse was that, a rugged tree and shrub grown rock rising on both sides with a saddle shape dipping in the middle.

While a few trails lead to Wild Horse Mesa, she'd learned from those who lived in the Canyon Mesa townhouses that it was fun to take Lookout Drive to an opening that led to the wide meadow where she could walk to the foot of Wild Horse. The way up challenged many hikers since they found no clear path and some slippery steep slopes that could cause a fall. She'd never fallen and didn't worry about it.

Not certain where she was headed, she looked across the landscape to find a point of direction so she could head back that way to get down, but no matter, she feared getting confused. Despite the concern, she tossed her head and wandered deeper onto the Mesa. As she walked, a silhouette appeared from the side, and she slowed. He must have noticed her too, but she could see no details.

The man veered a bit and headed her way, and though she'd always felt safe in Sedona, and especially the part called the Village of Oak Creek. The smaller community offered the comfort of a small town— restaurants, stores, and hiking trails that kept her from driving into the traffic of Uptown or West Sedona where the major stores were.

A faint sense of concern prickled down her spine, but as he drew nearer, a smile brightened his face. He raised his hand in a greeting, and she responded back, admiring his good-looks as he neared. "Hi. I didn't expect to find anyone here."

He shrugged. "I didn't either. I hadn't noticed anyone on the trails."

She motioned her hand toward her strange way of climbing to the top. "I took the non-trail route."

"Non-trail?" His eyes narrowed as his brow crinkled. "What's that?"

"I can show you if you want to see it."

His brow smoothed and his lips curved into a grin. "I'm always curious. Show me if you will."

She turned back, eyed her landmark, and made her way through the faint path to the spot. When they arrived, he gazed down the side of the rough mesa and shook his head. "You really climbed up that?"

"I did, and I've done it before. I live in Canyon Mesa, and this route is a sort of private way to get here and avoid the regular trails."

He moved closer and looked down. "Do you see that loose gravel? I'm surprised you haven't fallen. That looks dangerous to me."

"I like a little danger, I guess." Like danger? The comment was stupid. She feared anything she didn't know, even the stranger before she got a good look at him. "Perhaps that's a slight exaggeration."

"I hope so." He stood a while longer gazing out at the Canyon Mesa townhouses. "You should never climb alone especially when it's that rough." He turned and faced her. "You live in that community there?"

"I own a little casita."

"Casita?" His head tilted as he gazed at her.

"It's a smaller townhouse. Two bedrooms and baths but smaller rooms, and yet it's great for one person or even two if they don't mind spending time together."

He eyed her again and grinned. "I suppose that

depends on who the other person is."

She grinned back while admiring his light brown eyes like a fawn with specks of gold.

"I've noticed Canyon Mesa before when going up Jack's Canyon Road. It's gated, right?"

"It is, which helps me feel safe. The house belonged to my aunt who'd never married, and she treated me like the daughter she'd never had. She left the casita to me when she died, and I was touched since I love this area and always visited her when I could. I was born in Indiana. Much different than the southwest." She studied him a moment. "Do you live in Sedona or are you visiting?"

"I have a condo in West Sedona, but I enjoy some of the rock formations in this area so I come here to hike. It's not as crowded as some of the popular areas closer to Uptown."

"You have good taste."

He tossed his head back with his laugh. "Thank you...I think." His brow wrinkled again before he turned and extended his hand. "By the way, I'm Case Ashton."

She grasped his hand "Willow Randolph."

"Willow. That's an interesting name."

"Mom said I was a willowy baby, long and slim for a newborn. and I didn't flap my limbs like a baby. She said I looked like tree branches shifting in the wind." She shrugged having no idea where her mother had come up with all of that. "That's what she said."

"Then that's who you were, and you're still rather willowy. You're slender and seem to have long legs." He slapped his cheek with a grin. "Not that I'm ogling your figure. I noticed when you were further away.

That was my impression."

"Thank you…I think."

They both laughed, and she liked their common sense of humor.

"Do you mind if I walk with you?"

She studied him a moment, and liking him from the start, she agreed. "Which way?"

He motioned deeper onto the mesa, and though she had no idea where it went, she followed him. Though they walked in silence, he flashed her an occasional grin and slowed so she didn't have to struggle to keep up with him.

Though she enjoyed their silence, her curiosity won out. "What do you do here for a living? You're too young to be retired."

"I sure am, but I can do much of my work from home and I like the setup."

"Computer work, I assume."

He only nodded and pointed to the view. She stopped to admire the amazing view of the red rocks and pulled out her camera to capture a few pictures. While she did, she caught him in one, smiling at her, but she didn't tell him. Sneaking a photo seemed silly, but she wanted to keep the memory of the day with a stranger.

"Thanks for showing me all of this, Case. It's been fun, but I need to get back. I have a ton of things to do, and I'm working tonight of all things."

"Working? I wasn't thinking." He added his great smile. "Where do you work?

"At an arts and craft store in Sedona. My mother owned one, but wasn't a good business woman, and when she became very ill, I wanted to give her a hand so I worked the store and was there if she needed me."

"How's she doing now?"

"Mom died three years ago. I sold the building and stayed with my aunt, and then she died and left me the casita." She pointed toward Canyon Mesa, assuming she had pointed in the right direction. Getting turned around on the mesa made her realize that she needed to be careful when hiking. "I also had an interest in designing handcrafted jewelry and so I took a couple of classes and found I have a talent. Now I also sell some of my own work at the store."

"And on top of being determined and a hiker, I learn you're creative as well."

His look made her grin. "I guess so. I don't think creativity was in my family, but I got it from somewhere. Now I have no one to ask since mom and my aunt are gone."

"Then, you have no family here now?"

"None here or anywhere really, but I have a few friends in Sedona, and it's become home to me. I love the area…just as you do, I assume."

"You assume right." He gazed across the landscape for a minute before turning. "We'd better get you back, but I want you to come my way and not down that treacherous trail you climbed."

"But I don't have a car and—"

He rested his hand on her shoulder. "I have a Jeep, and I'll be glad to drop you off. It's on the way back."

"I guess that will work." Though taking the trail back down caused her no concern, she liked the man and going with him gave her a few more minutes to enjoy his company.

He beckoned her to follow and as they walked, she

admired his impressive build. He was maybe six feet tall, she guessed from her five foot seven frame, and his broad shoulders and chest tapered to a thin waist and long lean legs. Most of all, she loved his smile. Once she was on the trail, she couldn't turn back. "This trail is much longer than mine. We've been walking for twenty minutes and I don't see the parking lot yet."

"Patience. It's there. I suppose it is farther."

"A lot farther."

He patted her back and chuckled. "Think of the exercise and the new sights you're seeing."

"I can only think of two things. I've been duped and I'm really hungry."

"I can help you with the hunger part, but not your duped comment." He leaned over her with a wink. "I suggested we come this way, because I was thinking of your well-being. Someday you'll thank me."

"We'll see." She couldn't help but smile.

"And speaking of seeing." He pointed ahead of them. "See that speck in the distance. That's my Jeep in the parking lot."

♥

As he drove back toward Canyon Mesa, Case couldn't stop his concern for Willow. She insisted she could hike alone, but her determination worried him, especially on uncharted trails. Willow. He said her name over in his mind. The name suited her. Willows had slender limbs, and yet sturdy wood, though it was pliant. Willows had roots that went deep, and they were aggressive, often clogging drains. As he looked at her, the truth reminded him that she had already clogged his mind with an interest he couldn't control or, maybe, didn't want to.

"We're almost back. How about going to a restaurant. I could eat too. I'm getting hungry."

"I have food at home, but thanks." She turned and looked out the window in silence.

Unexpected disappointment struck him, but he let it go. He'd visit the store and see her one day, he hoped.

Though still looking out the window, she presented an offer. "Actually, Case, I have plenty if you'd like to join me." Finally, she turned. "Anyway, you can see what a casita is. You sounded as if you didn't know what they were."

"I'd never heard the term." His pulse skipped. "Are you sure I won't be in the way?"

"In the way?" She chuckled. "It's big enough for two people. I—"

"I didn't mean your home. I meant your sharing your lunch."

A smile curved her lips. "Oh, I thought... No, I have plenty, and you'd be very welcome to share."

"Okay then. That sounds good."

As he curved the road, he spotted the entrance to Canyon Mesa, and he turned through the gate and waited for directions."

"Make a right, and at the fork continue right onto Copper Springs."

He followed her directions and in moments, she had him pulling into a parking space. He turned off the engine and headed for the passenger door, but she beat him to it and beckoned him to follow. The beige stucco homes along the street were neat with an occasional flowering tree or shrub. "It's well-kept. Very nice."

"Thanks. We have maintenance people who keep it looking that way." She motioned for him to follow as she climbed the few steps. "Here we go." She unlocked the door and pushed it back for him to enter. He walked inside to an open floor plan with a small kitchen with an island that divided the area from the dining table and then the living room that stretched to a large window in front. He could see a broad green landscape. "Very nice."

"The view out the front window is part of the golf course—the second tee."

He looked again and notice the flag. "That's handy."

Willow motioned toward a doorway off the dining area. "To the right is a hall that leads to the bedrooms and bathrooms."

Though it was roomy enough, he couldn't help but compare his home in West Sedona and wondered what she would think. He didn't like his answer. "You are right. There's plenty of room for two people here."

She nodded but appeared preoccupied as she dug into her refrigerator. "I hope you like salad."

Salad? He ate salads that accompanied dinners, but what could he say. No wonder she had such a trim figure. "I enjoy a good salad." Too late to bite his tongue. Why did he add good to the salad comment?

"I'm glad you do. That's what I planned." She pulled out a stool beside the island. "You can sit here, or in there if you like."

Though she'd pointed to the living room, he pulled out a stool and sat. As she worked, his surprise grew. This wasn't an ordinary salad. She'd added meat and cheese and finally he realized it was more like an antipasto salad than a plain dinner salad. "It looks delicious, Willow."

"Thanks." She didn't look up but continued to add

olives and small light green peppers.

Once she'd tossed the salad, she plated it in colorful pasta-type bowls and pulled out bread sticks from a cabinet. "What would you like to drink?

"Water's fine."

She nodded and pointed to a nearby cabinet. "Glasses are in there. Water's in a pitcher in the fridge."

He followed her instructions, and instead of eating on the island, she motioned him toward the dining room table. He carried the water glasses and settled across from her at the table that already had placemats arranged for four. He wondered who she might have entertained.

The delicious salad won his award for the best antipasto salad he'd eaten, even in some of the restaurants. The flavors melded together heightened by the dressing she'd used. She seemed in thought, and he would have loved to listen to those ideas rattling in her head. "Are you thinking about work?"

She glanced his way, her head shaking. "I started a bracelet using cat's eye, and now I'm thinking to highlight it with a few amber beads to bring out the flecks of yellow."

When she lifted her head and searched his eyes, he longed to know why. "I like the idea. How did that idea come into your mind today?"

Willow squirmed in her chair as if uncomfortable, but that made no sense. It wasn't a personal question.

She remained silent as a pink glow enhanced her fair skin. Finally, she tilted her head and looked at him. "Your eyes."

His eyes? His mind shot back to his question. "I don't understand."

"Your eyes are a soft brown flecked with yellow highlights. The color is intriguing."

He didn't get that either, but he was glad his eyes offered her a creative idea. "I suppose I should look at them." He grinned, but she didn't grin back.

"They're different...beautiful to me. I think the sunlight brings out the yellow, but I noticed when something interests you, that amber color is more noticeable." Finally, she grinned. "You could give yourself away, you know." She leaned closer and nodded. "Right now, there's no sun, but the color is amazing."

Her warning sounded in his head. Give himself away. Is that what he was doing now. Did his interest in Willow act like a neon sign on his forehead? And he had no recourse other than to wear sunglasses or not look at her.

"Did I embarrass you? If I did, I'm sorry. You asked and I—"

"Not embarrass. You surprised me. I've really never paid attention to my eye color. They're just my eyes. Now yours are very pretty too. I noticed when I saw you on the mesa."

"Plain old blue. Nothing fancy."

"Not so. They're blue but they have a touch of violet in them. Like the flowers."

She touched her eyebrow as she gazed at him. "Not like the flowers. Like the old movie star Elizabeth Taylor. I've seen photos of her with eyes that color. She was one of my mom's favorite movie stars."

"I've heard that too." He shook his head. "Not about your mother but about Taylor's eye color."

She laughed, and the sound surprised him. Today

she'd seemed more serious at times, although she did make him laugh when they were on the mesa. Her manner fascinated him though he wasn't certain why. He set his fork in the bowl and moved it to the side. "I should be on my way, and I know you need to work. I'm interested in seeing some of your handcrafted jewelry, so don't be surprised if I stop by one day. I have a gift to buy, and one of your pieces might be perfect."

"I'll give you a business card for the store." She rose and headed into the living room, and when she returned, she handed him the information.

"Thanks." He slipped it into his pocket, grasped his bowl and headed for the kitchen.

"Don't bother, Case. It'll only take me a minute to clean up, and I don't mind at all. It was nice having you join me for lunch."

"My pleasure, Willow. You're a good chef."

She grinned and color rose up her cheeks again.

He backed toward the doorway. "I'll see you soon, and meanwhile, be careful where you're hiking. If you want company, give me a call." He paused a moment to dig for his card. "It's my private number so call anytime." He gave a quick wave and opened the door. As he stepped outside, he looked back over his shoulder. "Thanks again."

He hurried down the steps, almost hating to leave her behind. She'd made a difference in his day, and it's a day he would remember.

Lost In Red Rock Country

Made in the USA
Monee, IL
14 December 2020

53138426R00132